A Life's Wager
The Story of a Viennese Civil Servant

Studies in Austrian Literature, Culture, and Thought

Translation Series

General Editors:
Jorun B. Johns
Richard H. Lawson

Georg Potyka

A Life's Wager
The Story of a Viennese
Civil Servant

Translated and with an Afterword
by
Todd C. Hanlin

ARIADNE PRESS
Riverside, California

Ariadne Press would like to express its appreciation to the Bundeskanzleramt - Sektion Kunst, Vienna for assistance in publishing this book.

.KUNST

Translated from the German *Lebenswette*
© Edition Atelier

Library of Congress Cataloging-in-Publication Data

Potyka, Georg, 1938-
  [Lebenswette. English]
  A life's wager : the story of a Viennese civil servant / Georg Potyka ; translated and with an afterword by Todd C. Hanlin.
      p.   cm. -- (Studies in Austrian literature, culture, and thought. Translation series)
  ISBN 1-57241-127-9
  I. Hanlin, Todd C. II. Title. III. Series.
  PT2676.O894313 2004
  833'.92--dc22
                                                        2004048136

Cover Design
Art Director: George McGinnis

Copyright ©2004
by Ariadne Press
270 Goins Court
Riverside, CA 92507

All rights reserved.
No part of this publication may be reproduced or transmitted
in any form or by any means without formal permission.
Printed in the United States of America.
ISBN 1-57241-127-9 (paperback original)

1

Wide-open mouths towered above him, a mountain of mouths, so many you couldn't count them all. They blocked his path. If you stumbled onto them, you froze in your tracks, because if you so much as breathed you might make the mouths start chewing and devouring and make the mountain start to creep closer. He could stare at them forever, and that would keep the mouths closed forever, but he would never be able to move again. Only when his mother called him could life resume and turn the mouths to stone. He climbed over them with one step. Then he was standing by a pond which was bordered by stones, and in which two animals, which consisted almost entirely of pointed beaks, swam toward each other. They were called *Mauen*. He never found out what would happen if they touched each other, because with his next step he cleared the pond entirely. An arm came out of nowhere and struck at somebody. He avoided it. A little fish swam out of the mouth of a larger one, the larger fish chased it; meanwhile a school of tiny fish attacked the larger one from the side. He had to walk through a gray desert, past two cat heads as big as a man that stared off into space; a cloud passed overhead; an animal with a wide face sniffed an animal with a narrow face; he had to step over a snake; an army of ants surged toward him, but before the first one could touch him, he spread his wings and flew away. He landed on a field of gravel and had to wind his way through a gorge until he came to a broad, hospitable plain and could breath easier – he was back home.

That's the kind of thing you experience when you're barely three feet tall and crawl on all fours up the granite steps to the front door, while you gaze at the steps' gray speckles.

After a trip like that it felt so good to enter the cozy dark entryway, to hear the wooden floorboards creak under your feet, and come to the kitchen door. The aroma of different foods wafted out. It didn't smell like any one thing, but like all the meals that had ever been cooked there, along with their ingredients: like the lard which was kept in a jar in the pantry and turned up in almost all the other foods; like the basket with onions below the lard jar; like the grease on the wall above the oven; like the milk can which stood on the kitchen windowsill in the winter and in the pantry in the summer; and like the soap powder which his mother used to wash the dishes day in and day out. And he felt even better when he went through the kitchen into the nursery. This was a small room, but it contained a huge world. He could feel warm and secure on the brass cot back in the corner, but also uneasy at night when a black rooster sat at the foot-end of the bed. The best thing to do was not to look at it, but call for help from the Seven Dwarves. When they came, the rooster would fly away. Under the bed was America. When he put on his feather headdress and crawled under the bed, he was an Indian in his teepee. Beside the bed was a small, low chest where he stored his building blocks, his picture books, a hay wagon with two horses, and other neat things. Under the window across from the bed was a small table and an armchair securely fastened to the table. He sat there with his crayons and drew giants and dwarves, railroad trains puffing smoke, horse-drawn carriages, houses with doors, windows and chimneys, and fairytale castles. In the corner, between the toy chest and the table, was Africa. A black doll in a little velvet jacket was sitting there. On top of the chest, a white teddy bear sat on his throne. That was the North Pole.

Out in the kitchen his mother rushed back and forth between the oven, kitchen table, and the credenza, sometimes disappearing into the pantry. She sliced potatoes, onions, and green vegetables, stuffed meat through the grinder, and stirred around in pots. Little by little he realized there was more here than met the eye, things which he gradually discovered. The things his mother cut and stirred were bought from the grocer a few houses down the street. On the sidewalk children were running around and playing with a rubber ball. In the store women were waiting, jostling each other. From between their skirts and coats he could see the grocer putting cartons, paper bags, and cones made out of rolled-up newspaper into mother's shopping bag, then reach for the money she was handing him. "Where does the grocer get the potatoes?" he asked his mother as she was dicing the peeled potatoes. "They grow in the fields." "Do they grow on trees?" "No, they grow in the ground." "Why don't they grow on trees?" "Just because. Don't you know that curiosity killed the cat!"

"I've got to go shopping now." "I've got to cook now." "I've got to clean up now." That's what his mother always said when he asked her if she wanted to build a king's castle with him or go to America. But he also had things to do. "Poldy, straighten up now, we're going to eat soon!" she would say in the evening, and if he kept on building, he would soon hear: "Straighten up right away, or else you'll get a few swats on your behind!" If he still didn't do anything other than put three rocks in the box and run his train from America to Africa – with an uncomfortable feeling, of course – his mother would soon come back into the room. Her footsteps more resolute than usual, she would take him by the hand, and the castle, the train, Africa and America were left behind. His soup bowl was waiting on the kitchen table. And sometimes...the *boogieman*. The *boogieman* could come if he didn't put his toys away, if he took a knife from the table, played around with a light bulb or sat in front of his plate, chewing endlessly. "What does the *boogieman* look like? Does he look like the coal bucket?" "No, he's even bigger and blacker."

It wasn't pleasant to know about the *boogieman*. If you kept asking about him, you found out all kinds of horrible things. But the boy was cautious and furtively kept an eye out for him everywhere it was black: behind the cellar steps, in the coal buckets and the large locked chests, and in the little box next to the circuit breakers and fuses. One day his mother asked: "Poldy, I've got to get something from the attic. Do you want to come along, or are you going to stay down here all alone?" Stay down here, all alone with the *boogieman*? But what if he was up in the attic, too? "Is the *boogieman* in the attic?" "If you're a good boy, he won't come out." His mother grabbed two bags with old boxes and other junk and went on ahead. Poldy followed her over granite gorges and ravines that he had never crossed or climbed, he avoided new mouths and glaring eyes. The steps ended at an iron door. His mother unlocked it, opened it, and disappeared behind it. He hurried to follow her. His mother kept going on ahead, looked back, turned a corner...and was gone! All that remained was darkness, all the way up to the ceiling, separated by beams that collided with each other, trailed off into lateral passages, old furniture which stretched their legs helplessly into the air, chests with locks and iron straps, isolated from a rust-black wall behind them which was partitioned by a chimney, like two glaring eyes on both sides of an elephant's trunk. Was this where the *boogieman* was hiding? Was he in one of those chests? And suddenly the boy knew: the attic itself was the *boogieman*! Its darkness was alive, it reached out for him, out of the rafters, with countless arms, and the iron door had already swallowed him. Now in the jaws of the *boogieman*, he screamed. Fleeing in panic every which way in all directions, he threw himself on the floor. That moment lasted an eternity. "For Heaven's sake, what's going on?" His mother was there, took him by the hand and pulled him along with her.

"Were you afraid?"

He sniffled and nodded.

"But you don't have to scream like that! After all, you're a big boy now! Just look how dirty you are!"

He didn't say a word, because he still didn't feel back to normal just yet.

Aside from the doors to the vestibule and to the nursery at the back, the kitchen had another door. When he went through this door, something special happened – he was standing on his own mirror image. He could see how his own shoes were braced by the shoes from below – the rest was blurred, but he was still there. And with every step he took on the sea of polished wooden waves which promptly parted, the shoe from his mirror image always came from down below and held him up so that he didn't sink. Nevertheless he was happy when, after only three steps, he came to the shore where many flowers blossomed and intertwined behind a red border. Here he could look and smell, because it didn't smell like lard and celery, but like the gloss on the floor, like carpet, like a bookcase full of books, like a table and six chairs with turned legs, like an armchair and a sofa in the corner with a lamp between them, and like a small piano where he could make notes by pounding on its keys. But best of all was the bay window when the sun shone in through its panes. The path of the sunshine was indicated by tiny particles of dust which floated and whirled, intermingled, as it shone on the leaves of the plants on the table under the window, on the waxy-smelling sea, and on the flower land with the red border. "Poldy, what are you doing in there? Be a good boy and go to your room!" his mother would call out from the kitchen. He could tell what was coming. When her voice sounded firm, he would turn around, leave, and close the door behind him. But sometimes her voice sounded different, so that he dared to ask: "May I look out the window a little while?" Then his mother would come in, shove the flower table aside and put a chair by the window. Then he would climb up on the chair, crouch on his knees and look down at the women in the street as they went about their shopping, see two horses pulling the bread wagon, hear the honking taxis that looked like little black boxes on wheels – and they were called taxis because thumbtax were hidden inside them; and he really enjoyed it when the coal dealer's horse cart clattered over the cobblestones or when a three-wheeled delivery van jounced past.

Then at some point his mother would call him to lunch. And by the time he had finished his plate, the sun had disappeared from the bay window. The room didn't appeal to him anymore. Only when it began to get dark outside did the room become interesting again, because that's when his father came home, greeted him wearily, hung his coat on a coat hanger in the entryway, put on his lounging coat and slippers, and sat down in the armchair. And after his father had sat there for a while, the boy was allowed to approach him. Then his father's broad face with the high forehead would break into a smile, and he would hold out his foot so the boy could climb up and ride it. His father's name was Alois Navratil, and he worked for an insurance company. When he insured people, nothing bad happened to them. He knew everything the boy asked him. "Is there anything else besides Africa and America and the North Pole?" "Yes, we live in Europe." "Yes, I know that – but besides Europe?" "There's also Asia and Australia." "Where is Asia and Australia?" "Asia is right next to Europe, not very far from us. Australia is far, far away, on the other side of the earth." "Are there Indians in Asia, too?" "No, but there are Mongols there, and they look very similar to Indians. And some of them even ride small shaggy horses like the mustangs." "Do they also have headdresses like the Indians?" "No, but they have yellow-brown skin, broad cheekbones and slanted eyes." "Just like you?" His father smiled: "Not exactly. Their skin is even more yellow, and their slanted eyes aren't gray-blue like mine, but black. Their eyes are even more slanted. Like this!" And with his fingers his father pulled the corners of his eyes apart. "But maybe there is a slight resemblance."

"Do the Mongols also tie up their enemies at the stake?"

"No, but they do kill them. Fifteen hundred years ago a Mongol tribe, the Huns, spread throughout our region on small, shaggy horses, armed with bows and arrows like the Indians. These Huns destroyed all the villages and towns and killed all the people. They roared in like a storm from the broad plains of Asia, small and ferocious, and no one could stop them. So they devastated the whole countryside until they themselves were defeated by the last Roman troops."

The next day Poldy placed a footstool next to the window in the nursery and looked down into the courtyard. The ground was black and full of small stones. A pear tree stood in one corner. Covered with sparse climbing ivy, the walls of neighboring houses flanked the courtyard on three sides. At the back, where it bordered on the courtyard of the neighbor's house, it was sealed off by planks painted green. That was Asia over there.

When his father inspected himself more reverently than usual in the shaving mirror that hung in the kitchen from a hook on the interior window casement; when he scraped the foam from his neck and chin; when his mother didn't just wash her face and hands in the washbasin on the iron tripod in the kitchen, but locked herself in the kitchen wearing her dressing gown, only to reappear a while later with a fragrance; when his father didn't wear his gray pin-striped suit, but dressed in his Styrian suit with the stag buttons on the green lapels; when his mother stood before her dressing table and elaborately curled her hair, the folds of her dressing gown flowing about her, the fairest woman in the land, like the queen in the story of Snow White; when she laid out a fresh shirt, fresh socks, and fresh underwear for Poldy to wear, and then put a long braided bun with raisins on the table – that meant it was Sunday.

When they had finished the bun, they set off to church. His father went down the stairway first, Poldy followed him as fast as he could, his mother behind him. On the third from the last step on every landing he would call out: "Papa, catch me!" And his father would turn around and let the boy leap into his arms. On the street Poldy was allowed to walk between his parents, holding hands with his father and mother, sometimes exuberantly lagging behind. His parents would swing him forward so that he flew between them and landed a step ahead of them, until his mother stumbled in her high heels. When he had walked and flown a while, his mother would say: "Now, be a good boy!" And in a dense crowd of people in their Sunday best, he entered a wondrous world where everything was different than anyplace else: Saints from Heaven floated in the air, some supported by angels, some caught in a beam of light, others raised on high at the sight of God. After he observed them for a while, bells would ring, the organ would begin to play, and a tall priest, followed by several smaller priests, all in glorious vestments, entered the church.

Poldy sat quietly beside his parents and tried to pick out his playmates from among the angels and saints.

"Papa, why does St. Leopold have a flag and a crown?" he whispered.

"Because he is a duke – a prince."

"And why does he have a church in his hand?"

"That is the Klosterneuburg abbey which he founded."

"Did he also fight against the Huns?"

"No, he fought against others. But I'll tell you that later. Now be nice and quiet!"

Sunday noon, after dessert and coffee, the family set out for the streetcar stop. A flash of red, its bell ringing, the tram came into view, promising a great adventure. Poldy climbed up the steps and sat down on the light brown varnished wooden bench until a grown-up got on – children had to make room for them. Then Poldy stood in the middle of the car, held tightly to the bench, and envied the tall people who could hold onto the leather straps attached to the ceiling of the car. Then, when the conductor called out: "Last stop, everybody out!" he leaped down from the streetcar steps and followed his parents between fences, grass and trees, up a hill, all the while clattering a stick against the fence posts. When the fence ended, they came to a small grove of low, gnarled oaks, some of which were easy to climb. In a clearing he saw several brightly painted merry-go-rounds with horses, ducks, and elephants you could ride, also one with seats suspended from chains on which the more courageous children could fly around in a circle for the duration of a waltz played on a barrel-organ.

"Papa, I need a flag! Please make me a flag!"

His father tied his handkerchief to the stick. After riding on the merry-go-round with his fluttering flag, little St. Leopold ran to the edge of the meadow where he could look down the slope and out onto the plain, all the way to the range of hills in the Leitha Mountains, hidden by a haze that obstructed the view further off into the distance. They were way out there, the slant-eyed horsemen. They came over the hills on small shaggy horses so they could flood onto the plain. Duke Leopold waved his flag and ran to the brink of the perimeter of safety cast by his parents up above him. And with that the foe vanished into the haze.

A green plank separated his courtyard from the neighbor's. Starting in springtime, this was his favorite place to play. Leopold climbed up on the lower of the two beams of squared timber that held the boards of the plank together and peered over. A boy with straw-colored hair hanging down over his face was throwing little stones at a lump of soil.

"Hey, what are you doing?" Leopold yelled.

Without answering, the boy stared at him with watery-blue eyes... and then threw a stone at him! Leopold jumped down to the ground, picked up a handful of stones, climbed back up on the beam and threw the stones at the other boy. Without saying a word the boy picked up a fist-sized clod of dirt and heaved it at Leopold, just missing his head by an arm's length. Then the boy ran over to the plank and started pounding on it with both fists.

By the time he was bigger, he walked through a doorway which was taller than the doorway at home, and he had to climb three steps to get to it. Above the doorway a flagpole towered over him. Once inside, he had to climb a couple more steps, go around a corner and down a long hall. It was fun to race along the hall because, as you ran, you could come up behind one of the many smaller children and smack them on their book bag so that the buckle rattled. In the classroom there were friends and enemies, and he tried to find a safe place between the two parties. Then the bell rang, the teacher came into the room, and everybody had to be silent and write carefully in their notebooks. The next time the bell rang, they all stormed a door that smelled pungently like black oil and other stuff, to gain some mental and physical relief. Here, and only here, peace reigned. When you had shoved your way to the black-oiled urinal you were safe until you had relieved yourself. Afterward, outside in the hallway, your pants slightly damp, you could rejoin your friends, show a smaller kid who was boss, or get out of the way of a bigger kid until the bell rang again. This time no one was glad to hear it, and they all pushed their way back into the classroom.

During dictation, Poldy tried to imitate the teacher's voice with bows and loops on the paper. And when the teacher turned his back on them for just a second, a head from the seat behind him suddenly inserted itself over his shoulder, exhaled on his hand as it wrote, tickled him with greasy straw-colored hair, and peeked at what he had written with watery-blue eyes. "Teacher, Engelhofer is copying off my paper!" called out the student who had been interrupted in his writing. By that time Engelhofer was back slaving over his notebook, copying down whatever it was he had seen. Not wanting to encourage such tattling, the teacher ignored the complaint and got Engelhofer's attention with a stern look. But when the teacher had turned his back a second time, Engelhofer once again shoved his way between the students in the front row and stole the correct spelling from them as if it belonged to him. He had to steal, because a glance in his notebook revealed a horde of mongooses in red ink with a death grip on a gob of horribly twisted snakes in blue ink. In answer to the teacher's questions, his words were like fists, punching against a wooden plank. And after school, when someone cringed because someone else had shoved a dumpling-size wad of paper down the back of his shirt, then it was Engelhofer who was running off down the street. The boy who fished the paper wad out of the back of his shirt was seized by a special kind of rage – rage at the aggravation, and rage that the cowardly culprit didn't even grin shrewdly, but had the same old unchanged expression on his face that in no way was meaningless in its lack of expressiveness: "I don't know anything about it, and I don't want to know anything about it," his expression said to the investigating teacher. "Show me right now how to write that!" his expression demanded of his fellow student. And communicated it to the surprised student in such a way that behind his utterance lurked a violent deception which wouldn't betray itself with a grin or a four-letter word. Leopold, the warrior, duke, and saint, then ran after his abuser, caught him with a glancing blow as he ducked, and then ran off down the street himself, just barely avoiding the shopping bags of several corpulent women, and on around the corners of two or three houses.

> "A bag in his right hand,
> A package in his fist,
> A bald spot on top,
> Here comes our catechist."

The Reverend Wiesmüller, the religion teacher, would tell all kinds of stories about the Lord, about the creation of the world in seven days, about the Israelites' passage through the Red Sea, about Kings David and Solomon, and about the kingdoms of Israel and Judah. After they had said the Lord's Prayer together at the end of the class, Leopold was almost knocked to the ground by a cowardly punch, and Engelhofer yelled out: "Croak, Jews!" Leopold, who thought that meant an attack by the kingdom of Israel against the kingdom of Judah, screamed: "Croak, Israelites!" and punched him back.

The towers and cupolas of Klosterneuburg with its ducal hat and imperial crown soared high above the treetops in the forest meadow. With all this in front of him and his retinue from the seventh grade behind him, a fellow could leisurely stroll along, take possession of the countryside, and all the while wear a slyly pleased grin as his heraldic shield.

"This is the Leopolds' road," Leopold announced to his classmate Norbert Greiner who was walking beside him, silent and thin. "Here the Leopolds marched along the Danube at the head of their loyal retinue, drove out the Huns, built castles, founded monasteries, proclaimed Christianity, all the while acquiring for themselves a terrific duchy. They also built all that up there, and you iconoclasts wanted to tear it all down." He pointed to the abbey.

"None of that was built yet at the time of the Reformation, so we couldn't have torn it down. Besides, it was Adalbert the Victorious who conquered this region – and not from the Huns, from the Hungarians."

"Adalbert was an honorary Leopold, and the Hungarians are honorary Huns. And the towers and the Verdun altarpiece were definitely standing at the time of the Reformation."

"If we had wanted to destroy the towers and the Verdun altarpiece, then we certainly could have done it. But we left them standing," Greiner defended himself with his crooked mouth, which he seldom opened. But when he did open his trap, it made you want to shut it right away.

"Even if you didn't destroy it, you never would have been able to build it in the first place."

"That's because we built other things instead. After all, you don't have to embellish and gild the whole world."

"We don't embellish and gild anything at all. But for Christmas we get golden Christmas tree bonbons, and you guys get pinecones baked in bear grease for Yule-tide."

"We do so have Christmas trees, just like you, and just as good bonbons on them. And besides, it's okay to live a little in touch with nature and the people." The pinecones baked in bear grease didn't intimidate Greiner.

"We Catholics live much more in touch with the people than you.

The Catholic lifestyle is the lifestyle of the German people." He knew that for sure, from a reliable source.

"Yes, but it's a question of whether that's good or not. And all of our ethnic customs are purely Germanic."

"But if we Catholics didn't model them for you, you would have forgotten them a long time ago. Do you think the German people could have survived for very long if their highest sentiment had been burning their feet over the summer solstice fire or running through villages with Hitler, blessing the houses like the mythical *Perchten*? When faith is missing, everything becomes a circus, and sooner or later nobody is interested anymore!" Greiner, surprised by so much fervor, stared silently ahead for several paces, and for his troubles got bashed again: "And when were the German people more ethnic – before Luther or now? And after all, wasn't it the German people who built the Baroque churches? If somebody tries to tell you otherwise, he's lying!"

Greiner was silent for a few more paces. The Au forest told him he was right, and so he announced in conclusion: "No matter what, people don't need to go around building churches everywhere." People really *don't* need to do that, so it wasn't necessary to respond to Greiner.

"Front of the line, stop! We're taking a break," the history teacher called out from the rear; he had just been talking recently in class about the Reformation and iconoclasm. "Break-time!" the art teacher also called out, a teacher who enjoyed talking about the influence of the Baroque on folk art. A meadow lay before them. They all sat down in the grass and got sandwiches out of their backpacks. Leopold was mad that he had let Greiner have the last word, and he was really tempted to pound him with a couple of Eternal Truths. But he jumped up when a soccer ball hit him in the head. Of course it was Engelhofer who ran off with a stupid grin on his face. Leopold grabbed the soccer ball, chased after Engelhofer and hit him in the back of the neck. Then they both went off in opposite directions, swearing at each other.

After the outing they took a train back into the city. Leopold and some of his classmates went to a restaurant near the Franz-Joseph station. Engelhofer was also among them. Over a beer, Leopold told stories about Handsome Herbie and his girls. Everyone knew that Engelhofer had already had a great deal of success with girls, and everyone but him knew that his girls were nothing but tramps. So Engelhofer grinned when his classmates laughed, partly flattered, partly uneasy because he didn't know for sure how much of their laughter was at his expense.

No one could stroll down the marble corridors at the university quite so grandly as the student Leopold Navratil, shoulders forward, belly out, as he wandered over to his friends leaning against one of the arched windows, in order to "cauterize" one of them, as he called it. In the Catholic student fraternity *Vogelweide* they called him "sneaky Pete," because no one grinned as slyly as he and could play up to someone so nonchalantly and then sneak away after he had schmoozed a while with them. He greeted his friends with a grin: "So, here they all are..." and the others grinned back. The "others" were Philipp Mattauer, an unruffled, friendly picture book Easter bunny with an oval face that always looked amused because of his highly arched eyebrows. Beside him stood the colossus Ulrich Hornik who followed the world's progress through eyeglasses.

"So, how are things with our Handsome Herbie? Germany, awaken!"

That was meant for his fellow student Herbert Engelhofer who was standing with some other student at one of the nearby windows. In response to this greeting, Engelhofer cast an apathetic glance in Leopold's direction. When he turned his head, you could see a dueling scar on the left side of his face.

"And here comes our Statue of Liberty!"

The Statue of Liberty was the American student David Richardson, who slowly emerged from the lecture hall and surveyed his surroundings with the timid and inquiring glance of a stranger. Slender, blond, cute, he was highly appreciated by the coeds in the lecture halls, in the cafeteria, or in the standing room section at the opera, and was teased by some male classmates as their rival. But he paid no attention to either group. He slowly approached the clique at the window, and Leopold Navratil introduced him to his friends: "This is David Richardson. He has come from the United States to study how to solve problems."

Mattauer and Hornik shook hands with him, and Hornik asked: "What are you studying in our country, if I may ask?"

"I'm studying economics at your School of Marginal Utility with Professor Spann. They are extremely interesting people," David Richardson answered, all the while making every attempt to speak good German, which made him all the more likable.

"And you've got problems in the United States that you want to solve?" Mattauer asked.

"Yes, we've got problems. We've got a problem with unemployment and the depression, and we've got minors... ah, problems with minorities: problems with the Negroes, problems with the Italians, with the Jews..."

"The Jews are no problem for us, as you can see. They are just a problem to themselves," Navratil interjected. "And here comes our Jewish problem now!" He indicated another student, Bamberger, who stopped short when he heard this introduction. "First the Jews invented capitalism to go along with their unjustified profits, and now they're going to eliminate it with the aid of Austro-Marxism."

"Capitalism won't be eliminated either by the Jews or by the Austro-Marxists, but by the laws of history," Bamberger lectured.

"You see, that is the Jewish way. They sit back in their armchairs and let history work for them," Navratil snickered, and the others snickered with him.

Navratil glanced over to the neighboring window, to Herbert Engelhofer with the watery-blue gaze and to Tillman Petritsch with the steely glare. Bamberger walked off.

"Look, our neighbors over there have their own problems. They are of Germanic origin and their names are all Petritsch, Novak, or Horowitz."

"The Croatians are a Slavisized Germanic tribe, based on their language!" Petritsch shouted back.

"Yes, indeed, there are terrible communication problems among the Germanic tribes. They can't speak German, as you can see from their Führer's writings. And, based on language, their ancestors are a Slavisized Germanic tribe, a Hungarianized Germanic tribe, a Hebraeicized Germanic tribe..."

The group around Navratil laughed. Only David Richardson glanced back and forth from one group to the other, uncomprehending. Petritsch, two heads shorter than Engelhofer, stuck his chin out even farther than usual and yelled:

"We'll take care of your Jewish-Popish conspiracy soon enough!"

"We ain't worried," Navratil responded. "The Hebraeo-Marxists will bury you as petit bourgeois, and we'll say the last rites over your grave!" Having said that, with an imaginary monstrance he made the sign of the cross over the two neighbors. They didn't say anything after that. Meanwhile Leopold fired another salvo at the American: "You see, the Americans always try to convince everyone that they need their own car, then they have to work night shifts until everyone has a car. And finally they have to invent something so that the people don't actually drive all those cars, because otherwise there wouldn't be any room on the road for them all. For example, they tell everyone they should have a radio, so that they'll listen to the radio instead of driving their car."

"Yes, that's right, but that's not the problem. The problem arises when people don't have any more money to buy cars or radios – that's when we have unemployment," Richardson responded.

No one could come up with a rejoinder to that. Meanwhile it was time for the next lecture. The groups dissolved. Navratil put his hand on Hornik's shoulder and shoved him on ahead to the door of the lecture hall.

Alone, David went down the corridor, down the marble steps and into the courtyard. He sat down on the steps which led from the colonnade to the gravel path, leaned back against a pillar, gazed at the boring Renaissance façade on the other side of the gravel path, and replayed the just-concluded encounter scene by scene. In spite of the tranquility of the sunshine and the colonnade, he was restless. He tried to figure out why.

He had often seen students brawling among their various factions. And that they could fight each other for various reasons, even for their philosophies, and that such fighting could even lead to bloodshed – he knew all that from his own country. After all, he was familiar with the Ku-Klux-Klan. He didn't worry about the two men at the next window: the tall, clumsy guy who walked bent over, all the better to attack someone smaller, and the shorter, stocky guy who was constantly standing on his tip-toes so that he could look out over his fellow men. David could simply avoid them, and that was fine with him. If he had to talk to them, he would just walk right up to them and express himself concisely. But then there was this Leopold Navratil, on legs that looked as if he were straddling a horse, his knees and belly out like a garden gnome with a load in his pants – even though he wasn't small. And he performed an act, unfamiliar to David as a Protestant, which could only be a gesture of blessing – the sign of the cross was unmistakable. His stance displayed scorn and contempt. Only if you had a very low opinion of someone would you push out your belly and make a magic sign in his face and not take it seriously. But in spite of everything, this outrageous gesture had placated the two roughnecks better than he, David, could have tamed two bullies from the Ku-Klux-Klan with his upstanding attitude and clear speech. The Klanners would have continued to taunt him, trying to get him to lose his temper, but the German bullies had simply slunk off in response to Navratil's grimace. "The Hebraeo-Marxists will bury you as petit bourgeois, and we'll say the last rites over your grave!" Nobody liked to be called petit bourgeois, and there was nothing the two must have hated more than being buried by the Hebraeo-Marxists of all people – unless it was perhaps the thought of being given the last rites by this Leopold Navratil. And as for the Hebraeo-Marxist Bamberger, neither Navratil nor the other two thought much of him, even if each of them thought nothing of him for different reasons. The Hebraeo-Marxist had stopped near Navratil so that he could respond to his taunting. But when Navratil engaged the guy with sandy hair in conversation, Bamberger disappeared. After Pontius Pilate had interrogated and mocked Jesus, he sent him to Herod. And from then on, the two powerful men became friends, though they hadn't liked each other up to that point. "The Hebraeo-Marxists will bury you as petit bourgeois." By beginning the sentence with this contemptuous term, Navratil had made the two bullies his allies, only to be able to insult them with impunity with the rest of the sentence – "and we'll say the last rites over your grave." That was another step on the tightrope where a fellow could fall off on either one of two sides: into the fury of the two enraged bulls (since it was disgusting to be blessed by Navratil with a load in his pants), or into a fellow's own ridiculousness. But Navratil didn't fall. Apparently he didn't think he was ridiculous, and his friends would stand by him to the extent that they thought the two figures at the next window were more ridiculous than Navratil. At first, even David had been taken by surprise by this farce and could only now make sense of it. When he put the pieces back together just now, he was even more amazed at the brilliant constellation of abuse, contempt, submission, and alliance against a third party – and, yes, including the simultaneous threat of an alliance *with* the third party. Could all that co-exist side by side? Probably only if it wasn't really sincere to begin with. David believed in his friends and his country, in democracy, and in his enemies. He had gotten along peacefully with everyone at his college, but if he had ever had to face a provocation, he had been prepared to fight.

David studied the pebbles in front of him, the white lady sitting on her pedestal in the middle of the courtyard, and the other students sitting on the stone benches. The students talked with each other, ignored each other, liked or despised each other. David didn't know what motivated each individual student, but at the moment the students here in the courtyard seemed more at ease among their peers than he. And he realized that not everyone was like him. Not everyone thought it necessary and honorable to be the way he was. Not everyone stood fully and completely behind every word he spoke, behind every handshake he extended, behind every punch he threw or took. There were people who could leap around in their principles like a monkey in a cage – you couldn't pin them down anywhere at any given time – until the constant movement became a permanent condition.

David went to the snack bar, bought a small cup of black coffee and sat down at an empty marble table. He had once heard that the Austrians are a nation of headwaiters. As an economist he knew that could only be a malicious generalization, because for every headwaiter there had to be others to whom he could serve coffee. That was true in economics and also had to be true in a moral sense: the best and most profitable virtues of a headwaiter lost their value if there were no customers to pay for them.

But in the final analysis, even if an Austrian headwaiter was something special, someone who made you forget many other Austrians, and even if Leopold Navratil was something special, if for no other reason than because he gave David so much to think about – then wouldn't it be productive to combine these two phenomena he was pondering here in Austria and to make Leopold Navratil…a headwaiter? Yes, when David entered the restaurant, Leopold Navratil was standing by the door. bowing conspicuously. This approximated the anticipated order of a small cup of black coffee and the tip David would owe according to local custom.

A coed with a small cup of coffee came over from the snack bar, approached David, asked: "Is this seat taken?" and sat down at David's table. She had shoulder-length dark hair, and her pretty girlish face gazed at him. A blue dirndl with white dots suited her perfectly. She drank her coffee so unaffectedly that David had to stroke her cheeks with a few words:

"You're not Viennese?"

"How can you tell?"

"Your dress, for one thing."

"That's a Carinthian dirndl."

She mentioned that she was from Rosegg in the Rose Valley, and he told her that he came from Philadelphia and was studying political economics so that he could learn to solve his country's problems.

"You should be a king who tells people what they should do, or a president in America."

David felt like a crown prince or a presidential candidate, and before they left the table, each one had written down the other's name, address, and telephone number. Her name was Erika.

Erika felt good in her dirndl – it fit her perfectly and looked lovely on her. In the lecture hall she liked to sit next to Rosi Lemnitzer. Rosi wore a dark gray outfit – and it, too, looked lovely on her. Erika studied English so that some day in the future she would be able to cram it into her students' heads in school. Rosi was studying English to be able to communicate with Gainsborough and Turner in their mother tongue. There was always a sketchpad or an illustrated art history peeking out of her portfolio. When Erika sat next to Rosi, she took part in the world outside. And Rosi enjoyed cutting loose with a tirade – Erika could identify with some things that she herself had always intuited but had never put into words. Sometimes one of Rosi's crazy ideas would collide with Erika's horse sense, and then Erika could argue with her to her heart's delight.

On this particular day, when Erika entered the lecture hall for her English workshop, a cynical young wise man had propped his elbows on the desk next to Rosi. His narrow eyes and lips reminded her of a jeweler who was peering into the works of a watch, though his round cheeks and mischievously disheveled hair could have been those of a devil. Erika sat down a few rows behind the two.

"Modern art attempts to depict the essence of things – in other words, to make their heart and soul visible to the outside world," Rosi was just explaining.

"Modern art forces things into a straightjacket, so that you can't see anything of their outside and nothing at all about what's inside. Besides, what is 'the essence of things' anyway? What you see in Schiele's works, or in Kollwitz's or Picasso's? I went to an exhibition not long ago, and it was horrible, let me tell you, horrible!" And Leopold clamped his hand over his eyes.

"Everyone sees the essence of things differently. That's just it. If you're interested in what I see, then fine! Here is a drawing of my nude back. I drew it in front of a mirror." She pulled her sketchpad out from under her desk, opened it discretely, and let Leopold take a peek.

"Hmm! Rubens could learn a thing or two from you!"

"Do you really think so?" Rosi accepted the compliment (which she attributed to her artistic skill). At that point the instructor entered the hall and the class began translating a newspaper article into English.

After class, Erika pushed her way through the door, out into the hall, and hurried over to the blond young man who was leaning against one of the pillars between two windows, obviously scanning the crowd to find her. No sooner had the two of them smiled at each other, than Leopold and Rosi emerged behind her.

First they went to the student cafeteria for lunch. Leopold held Rosi back a bit until the two were out of earshot, and then he asked her: "Do you like him, the good looking young man?"

"Why shouldn't I like him? He's dashing. He looks as if he had been painted by Gainsborough."

"But you're not his type, you're just my type and nobody else's. In fact, I'm a fan of Rubens. I'm your only chance."

"What will you give me if I can make him fall for me?"

"I'll give you a pickled herring. And if you don't succeed, you owe me one."

When the four of them were sitting in the cafeteria with their sausages, Leopold began the conversation, since he knew that Rosi's parents had a tennis court next to their country house: "Our friend David is a great problem solver. But he also looks like a great tennis player."

"Well, not a great one," David protested.

"Of course he's a great one, he's just shy and won't admit it. You've overwhelmed him with your charms," Leopold countered, with a side-glance at Rosi.

"If you like, we can all play tennis together sometime at my parent's country home," Rosi suggested.

Two cypress trees flanked the garden gate and pointed to higher spheres. The gravel path slowly wound its way upward. Gravel crunching beneath their feet, they climbed higher, between the two treetops, sacred groves and South Sea Islands suggested by chalk cliffs with gentian, ginkgo trees, and azaleas. Erika knew the way, but every time she climbed the path it was with the same reverence, from wonderland to wonderland. On her right, Leopold walked with his knowing gaze, on her left, David, his facial expression an unvarying "Oh, I see!"

At the first bend in the path Rosi came to greet them, wearing a white blouse and a short tennis skirt. She led her guests to a gravel area where Papa and Mama Lemnitzer were drinking their coffee. Leopold greeted Mama, kissing her hand flamboyantly. "You kiss hands with a lot of salad oil," Rosi teased him. Then they walked past the villa and Erika, looking more at David than at the house, saw how he gawked, uncomprehending, at the colorful glass windows and the art nouveau ornamentation. The tennis court was located behind the house; nearby a table and four chairs with four coffee settings were already waiting. The maid promptly served coffee and pastry.

After their snack they played mixed doubles, with David and Erika against Leopold and Rosi. Due to Rosi's graciousness, Erika was able to make a couple of forehands, David saved her by taking the backhands. They could all recognize that Rosi had benefited from several dozen hours with a coach. The two gentlemen refrained from showing the extent of their skills. No one kept score.

After a while, Rosi suggested that the two ladies rest and the two gentlemen play a match against each other. Now it had come, the moment they had been waiting for – the girls sat down on the bench, Leopold chose his court, and David would serve. He positioned himself at the baseline, tensed his muscles, lofted the ball, reared back...and peppered the ball into the net. Erika felt sorry that his splendid serve fell short. Leopold smiled broadly. And this wasn't David's only fault: his style was impressive, but time after time his perfect shots were out. Leopold stood across from him with legs spread wide and returned the few good serves net-high, usually deep at David's baseline, once or twice just clearing the net. They came back at David soft and hard to handle, half potato dumpling, half meatball, and David flubbed them more and more frequently. Following one particular net ball, he mumbled an ungentlemanly English four-letter word.

David lost. After match point the two opponents met at the net to shake hands – Leopold, with his swaying sailor's gait, half-smiling, half-grinning. David approached this tennis monster reluctantly and clumsily, and stared at him as incredulously as he had at the art nouveau monster of a villa. In Erika's eyes he was a star pupil who had just been beaten up by the class bully. And Leopold really was the best kind of bully, with his grin, his disheveled hair, his squint – you had to hand it to him. David had come to solve problems. But here he had run up against a new one, and his helplessness didn't bode well for the solution of his other problems. Approaching the girls, his glance vacillated from one to the other. Erika looked him straight in the eye, but he didn't hold her gaze, because Rosi went to meet him and captured his attention; the little boy who had been beaten up had found a mother to console him. Erika's gaze moved on and found Leopold, happily grinning.

Rosi demonstrated her skills as hostess. She complimented David on his good play on foreign soil and predicted that in the future he would win regularly on this court after he became acclimated to his new surroundings. David dismissed this, saying that it couldn't have anything to do with the surroundings, they were absolutely lovely. With that, Rosi invited him to take a stroll through the garden, and they disappeared behind an oleander bush in the direction of the house. He wouldn't easily escape without first seeing her sketches of the garden trees and blushing at the sight of the drawing of her nude back.

Meanwhile Erika admired the successful tactician who had defeated the brooder, and answered all his questions about her favorite flowers, her hiking through the Nock region, and her favorite sights around Vienna. When Rosi and David reappeared from the house, they had made a date to go to a concert. Erika and Leopold, for their part, had planned an outing to the zoo in Sparbach.

In the sunlight the broad meadow flowed down to the valley. In the distance wave after wave of hills stretched to the point where the sky met the earth. The air was alive with chirping and humming, the city was far off.

They stood, breathing it all in, and gazed over the summer landscape, then sat down under the spreading limbs of a pine tree. Leopold opened the knapsack and offered Erika a sandwich that she had made at home, she poured him a cup of tea which he had brought in a thermos. After the meal, she leaned back against the tree trunk, stretched her legs out into a patch of sunshine, and pulled the hem of her dirndl a hand's length over her knees. When she casually lifted the neckline of her dress ever so slightly from her bosom to let the little breeze cool her off a bit, Leopold was overcome. He put his arm around her shoulder to kiss her. She offered him her cheek. They sat that way for a while: she was smiling, restrained; he was enthralled at the sight of her. Then she looked him in the eye and asked: "Shall we pick a bouquet of flowers?"

All about them bluebells, daisies, carnations, and many other more unassuming wildflowers were blooming. Each of them picked a bouquet, and then they sat down under the tree, side by side, to weave the two bouquets into one.

"When I was a child, I read a book that said an elf lives in every flower," she told him. "Each elf looks like its flower: the Turk's-cap elf has a red turban, the lily elf a white dress. The elf in the bluebell has a bell-shaped dress and rings a little bell when a storm approaches. I used to sit down in the garden in the meadow and listen to the stories the flowers told each other. At night, when the flowers close, the elves come out and dance on the meadow; when morning comes, they go back and hide inside their blossoms. When you pick the flowers, they wilt, and the elves die."

"Then we'll put a bowl of water next to the flower vase – the best thing would be some kind of green and white salad bowl from Gmünd – and when the elves get thirsty, they will fall in and be revived."

Just the thought of elves, happily fluttering in the salad bowl, made them laugh. "Near Augarten there is a shop that specializes in wildflowers, and one Christmas I gave my aunt a basket from them.

We could order a bowl from that same shop, and then the elves would feel right at home."

"Yes, that's a good idea. But a green ceramic bowl from Gmünd would do just as nicely."

He stood up and stretched. Here he stood, Leopold, the lord and master of her fantasies. He had dumped her elves into a salad bowl and she hadn't minded. The wonderland of her dreams belonged to Leopold.

They walked on, Erika still smiling to herself. Leopold put his arm around her waist.

That evening, when she had disappeared into the house, he leaped into the air and hurried home. He crossed the Ring and strolled down the narrow lanes in the inner city. From the Domgasse he approached the tower of St. Stephan's. He had often tested his courage by looking upward from the foot of the tower to its spire – every time he knew he would get dizzy. The tower began to sway and detach itself from its foundation, and its soaring limbs wanted to grab him and hurl him up, out into the sky. Leopold chanced another look, but lowered his eyes before he flew completely out into infinite space. He approached the tower and struck his hand against the cold stone.

Inside the university, you could study; outside, in the park at City Hall, you could think. The tops of the giant trees spread over paths and lawns. From his bench under the trees, a thinker could think thoughts, could look up and glimpse the ramifications of space and time, until he eventually focused on shapes that he could identify:

Over there, Engelhofer was tripping over his own feet. Someday he'll be fishing money out of Austria for his German brothers – for Krupp and for Herr Goering personally. He will formulate his legal briefs so clumsily that an adversary will only need to file for recognizance to win the case. I'm curious how long it will take before Engelhofer loses his first case against Bamberger, the Jew. Then there'll be a great buzzing in the German press. Afterwards Engelhofer will have to earn his daily sausage ration by attending Nazi demonstrations, throwing stones, and smashing windows.

I'd really like to see a trial where at least one of the two lawyers isn't a cutthroat. If, out of friendship, you don't sue in time, due to the statute of limitations you lose compensation for damages. If, out of tact, you don't cover your spouse with as much dirt as he or she throws at you, you lose your divorce case. In court a nice guy has to pick up the pieces in the name of God the Almighty, from Whom all justice flows.

I don't want to have to look the other way when I see somebody coming down the street, somebody whose child I've been fortunate enough to have taken away by the Court. The district judge in Gmunden couldn't look anybody in the eye after he had spent twenty years peering into everybody's dirty laundry. "Respectfully yours," the defense attorney writes to the sexual murderer and the court-appointed lawyer to the gangster. If the pack of criminals they represent is so respectable, then they are, too, and that reassures them. I don't have any respect for that kind of riff-raff, and don't want to be a judge who wallows in their muck until I myself fall in.

Thank God, there are other things lawyers can do. They can allocate, approbate, give and take, administer an estate. They can also regulate and accommodate. They've been doing that since time immemorial.

Wherever people gather together to do something constructive, somebody has to give the orders. Nowadays the people who do such things sit in district offices, police stations, and internal revenue offices, in magistrates and ministries. They stipulate taxes and reduce them, they permit and prohibit the opening of taverns and hotels, pave the way for streets, railroads, and water lines. Now and then somebody says "Thank you" to somebody for his trouble, and he's allowed to say "You're welcome, happy to do it." As a judge he couldn't do that – the eyes of Justice are blindfolded.

Is it possible that all that constant argumentation, raking in money, pitting one's strength against another's in court leads to some unknown goal? The lawsuits, counter-suits, objections, verdicts and resolutions, confiscations, insolvencies, and foreclosures – do they somehow come together like vault and abutments, do they form walls, pillars, arches, and stained glass windows which unite in a perpetually unfinished building, rising up to an abyss as high as the sky where you can't look up without becoming so dizzy that you have to close your eyes?

"Hey, Poldy! Are you daydreaming?" It was Philipp Mattauer.

"Yes, I'm daydreaming. And I've just found out that it doesn't agree with me."

Three months later Doctor of Laws Leopold Navratil and Doctor of Laws Philipp Mattauer were sitting across from each other at two desks in an office in a suburban district of Vienna, receiving petitioners, accepting petitions, and preparing legal adjudications which would allocate the state's property.

Commissioner Navratil, LLD. initialed the file and said: "There, that's that!"

"That's what?" Commissioner Mattauer, LLD. asked.

"An opinion on whether Herr Stone has to pay a fee for his petition. According to the judicial ruling from the Administrative Court, he has to pay it."

"You're working as a bloodsucking fee processor?"

"Certainly. If Herr Stone wants something, then he ought to pay for it, just like Herr Wood, Herr Field, or Herr Root. In the final analysis, we civil servants live off his money."

They enjoyed meandering over the Gmünd meadows of documents that sprouted in the names of real and imaginary petitioners Stone, Wood, Field, and Root. Mattauer smiled politely in the background, in his elegant suit that must have cost at least two months' salary. But when Navratil looked up, over his frayed shirtsleeves, he saw much more: Mattauer was smiling at the presumption that he would have to live on his civil servant's salary.

"I know you don't need to live off your salary, you can also live off your landed properties. And if you don't like it here, you can retire as a Styrian gentleman farmer and stroll along leisurely behind a plow."

Mattauer again smiled politely. "Yes, that would be a good idea." But as he said that, he had tilted his head just a bit too far back and raised his eyebrows just a bit too high. Navratil understood: civil servant Mattauer was smiling about civil servant Navratil. Mattauer was no gentleman farmer, he was a gentleman civil servant. He wanted to become head of a department, because that post offered such an interesting view of world affairs. Navratil would never be able to compete with him for that position: He would stipulate fees, fill out documents, and work himself up through the ranks. When Navratil the tortoise had reached his goal, sweating profusely, there, sitting in an elegant suit, would be Mattauer the hare smiling at him, without ever having had to move his hind legs: "I'm already here!" Others would vouch for him, not only his father, Department Head Mattauer, who hosted not only theater directors and famous artists, but occasionally also ministers who were flattered to be able to admire his collection of Chinese porcelain figurines; and his mother, whose maiden name was *von und zu Something-Stein* and who had brought a country estate with a castle to the marriage; but also Philipp Mattauer himself, who had forged a career path that Navratil couldn't follow. Mattauer played with his career, but he played for high stakes. He pursued his goal intently and openly, no matter what his father did behind the scenes to pave the way for him. He not only belonged to a pious and active fraternity, as Navratil did also, but, more importantly, he was a member of the Ostmärkische Sturmscharen, a conservative paramilitary organization in support of the Austrian government. Here his father could sponsor his protégé better and more openly, because personal reliance was the highest virtue, and for that reason he was already rather high up on the totem pole. If Navratil were ever to join such an organization, there, too, he would have Mattauer over him, smiling in a friendly manner at his political views. So there was no place for him there. Besides, the basic nature of such clubs was not his style; with his blatantly extended belly and particularly his drooping shoulders, which betrayed his true feelings for military life, he didn't fit in any military formation, not even in that of the Ostmärkische Sturmscharen. And what, exactly, did the storm troops want to storm? You would either have to have a wonderful imagination or none at all in order to overlook the fact that they were clay pigeons in a shooting gallery. Mattauer was probably one of those who had no imagination – whenever he imagined something, he could never picture something else simultaneously. He never knew necessity, which is the mother of invention. If something bad should happen to the Storm Troops, to the Patriotic Front, and to Austria itself, he could always live off his mother's estate. Even if people laughed at him in his uniform which made him look like a tin soldier, Navratil would rather laugh along than have people laugh at him as a person.

Navratil began to write on another file. After a while he had something else to say: "By the way, I don't see why I shouldn't work in an orderly juridical manner, since I am a lawyer."

"Do you call that legal work? That's enough to make the chickens laugh!" Mattauer joked.

"Of course I call that legal work, and that's just what it is. If you think that only *The Spirit of Roman Law* by Ihering is legal practice, then you're wrong. Nowadays we are the equivalent of the ancient Roman praetors. We have to make the law, and we don't need any Rudolf von

Ihering to do it. Of course you have to see the legal code in the context of everyday life, and to do that you have to know everyday life. A lawyer who is only a lawyer is a poor devil. By the way, I'm a very good lawyer!"

Mattauer swallowed his laughter: "I never doubted it for a minute," he assured him.

But something else occurred to Leopold: "It seems to me that my legal work is at least on the same level as your art of warfare."

"My art of warfare has no level at all. I simply want to be prepared, when the time comes. I try to conduct myself so that I can always hold my head up high, even when others are trying to bring me down."

"Just make sure you don't hit your head on the ceiling arches when you go down into your father's wine cellar."

"You'll see."

Y ou'll see.
Mattauer's words stayed with him. We'll see if Mattauer ever bows his head. It was clear that Leopold would bow his head, at least to get down into the wine cellar. Besides, he had tried to take Mattauer's proud assertion that he wouldn't bow before his enemies and get him down into the wine cellar. If Mattauer had simply smiled and said in passing "We'll see," then the two of them would have gone down the steps to the wine cellar arm in arm. But he had rebuffed Leopold and confronted him "You'll see." That meant, "You'll see which of us can keep his head held high longer." That was a wager, a wager that would last for many years, until one of them had laid his head to rest for good – a wager for a lifetime. He, Leopold, had provoked it with a feeble joke. Now the wager was on.

Once again the Gmünd meadow of legal briefs surfaced from the fog. Mattauer, in uniform and with a pistol in his hand, leaped up from behind Stone's stone, charged ahead, signaled a squad of riflemen to take the high ground, and took cover himself behind Wood's woods. The riflemen took their positions behind Root's roots and Field's tufts of grass. Shots rang out. Mattauer raised up and looked out over Leopold, out onto the battlefield, his forehead and cheeks creased. Gone was the Easter Bunny of yesteryear. He signaled to the riflemen and strode off to face the enemy, over Leopold's prone body.

This was the fellow Leopold had challenged.

"See you later," Mattauer said at four o'clock, and went off to his Sturmscharen.

"See you later, fight the good fight," Navratil replied, and kept writing in his files.

"Well, it's all over now," his father said, sank back down into his armchair and stared at the carpet in front of him. Leopold couldn't think of anything to say. "I'm just going up to the attic for a minute," he said.

He climbed the worn granite steps, opened the iron door and set foot in the space beneath the roof timbers; a few dying rays of sunlight forced their way through the chinks between the roofing tiles. As a child he had often ventured into this darkness to pursue his lurking fear. This fear had often overcome him and cleansed him of so much tangible dread – of having his ears boxed or of poor grades at school which had suddenly accumulated disastrously. Now he immersed himself once again in the darkness. He went over to the enclosure where his parents stored their junk, opened the attic window and looked out over the courtyard and the top of the pear tree, out onto the city. Swastika flags were flying from the roof of City Hall and from many other buildings.

As he left his office building, he had taken a look back, as if to ask how many more times he would come and go to work, because as a member of an active Catholic fraternity he was begging to get sacked, and sooner rather than later. Yes, I'll be the first to go, and Mattauer with me. Mattauer might even go before I do; on top of everything else, he was also in the Patriotic Front. Maybe they'll be satisfied when they've thrown him out, and they'll let me stay. Or they might let me stay, but since they've thrown Mattauer out, they'll have to toss me out with him. Then I can wash dishes at home. We now have a Thousand-Year Reich – I can wash dishes for a thousand years. Because Austria is only the beginning. All the neighboring countries will be next. Hitler will protect the Germans far and wide, and Germanicize the rest. We'll provide him with the ammunition. I'll stand on the assembly line, and every time I put together an artillery shell, I'll think: "The hell with it!" No, I won't furnish weapons for the German army purely out of gratitude because they've invaded us. I'll have to come up with some way out.

The view of the city with St. Stephan's in its midst used to be so beautiful! Today those Swastika flags are hanging everywhere. To cling to old appearances and pull yourself out of your present misery and project yourself into a happier time – it just doesn't work.

Maybe you could stick together with one of your fraternity brothers? The German-lover Greiner likes me. Right now he's probably standing up on the Küniglberg, listening to the German oaks rustling, feeling himself one with the German people. During Hitler's next conquest he'll be the first to die for the Fatherland. He won't be able to help me. But...why didn't I think of him right away! He's been living right next door for twenty years! What a catch! What a protector! When we were little kids we used to throw rocks at each other. If that's not a common bond, what is? He's stupid, but people like him are important to a political party, especially to a party like the Nazis. Yes, Handsome Herbie has got to save my job. Just before final exams I got into a fight with him and his German brotherhood. I really hit him a good one, but he got me, too – thank God. I just have to butter him up, everything else will take care of itself. The Swastika flags will deface the rooftops of Vienna for a while longer, but right now that's less of a problem. The birds crap on the rooftops, and it doesn't bother anybody. And even I will have to hang Swastika flags out my window. I'm willing to do that for them. I won't voluntarily register myself with the Gestapo as a "social parasite." They want to be buttered up, front and rear. I'm willing to do that for them, too. If they arrest me, they won't get me. They'll get to know the real me! No, they won't get to know the real me. I know them, and that's good enough.

It had become almost dark. Leopold went back downstairs and sat at the table. They talked very little, but his resolute attitude gave his parents a smidgen of solace and security.

He had the secretary announce his presence to Legal Clerk Engelhofer, LLD, and sat down in the waiting room. Adolf Hitler gazed down upon him from his picture frame. No matter what Leopold said to Engelhofer, he would also have to find mercy in Hitler's eyes. "You know you've always stood up for your opinions and I for mine..." That wouldn't help one bit. Whoever stood up for the wrong opinions was put in prison. "I think you know you can put your trust in me, a civil servant for whom his people and his country are paramount..." That didn't sound too bad, but each of them understood something different when it came to *his* people and *his* country. "Sometimes we've been on opposites sides, politically, but..." What could he say after that? "If you want to do a favor for an old playmate and school chum..." The word "chum" sounded phony – as soon as he said it, the lie became evident. He couldn't fool Engelhofer...and he didn't have to. Engelhofer didn't have to believe anything he said. He only had to want to believe it.

Dr. Engelhofer had him paged. The secretary held the door open, and Leopold entered. Sitting behind a mahogany desk, Engelhofer looked up at him with watery blue eyes. On the back wall of his office stood a worn-out but genuine leather suite of office furniture, between the two windows a small mahogany cabinet, behind the desk a larger one. The decor suited Engelhofer well – in this room he was a lawyer, from head to toe, the kind no one would ever have expected him to become. And even Adolf Hitler, who looked out over Engelhofer's shoulder from a metal frame atop the small cabinet – this was not the screaming proletarian. No, he was Adolf Hitler the author of the profound and fascinating work *Mein Kampf*; not Hitler the thug and con man, but Adolf Hitler the statesman who, with an iron hand, was leading an errant generation out of their sentimental humanitarianism toward becoming a new, dynamic human race. Not Hitler the would-be writer who didn't even know decent German, but Adolf Hitler the renovator of the German language based on the spirit of his accomplishments. Engelhofer and Hitler – they could both see clearly. And Leopold would have to be brief:

"Hi, Herbert! I just came to see you because they're probably going to kick me out of my office. You know me. I only need to tell you that I'm a conscientious civil servant who would continue to be an asset to the state. That's why I've come to ask if you could put in a good word for me upstairs, so that I can keep my job?"

Evidently Engelhofer didn't immediately comprehend what this was all about. It wasn't until the end of Leopold's speech that an expression suddenly crossed his face – that of a wolf, opening his jaws, just about to bite: you mean, I've finally got you? Engelhofer, with those watery blue eyes, needed a few seconds before he took charge. Then he asked: "Who?" This fellow and that one. "Good, I'll see what I can do." Only then did he rise from behind his desk, approach Leopold, and offer his hand in a solemn gesture. The wolf's welcome practically forced Leopold Navratil's upper body forward into a bow, and at the point where he was about to lose his balance, he even arched his neck and shoulders. Then he left the chancellery and absorbed the entire experience with a deep breath: "That ought to take care of that."

His way home led down the street past City Hall where Philipp Mattauer lived. His father, Department Head Mattauer, had a residence commensurate to his rank and social stature. A police car was parked in front of the Mattauers' house. Navratil approached the building from the other side of the street; from here he could see what was going on without coming into contact with the police. When he was directly across from the entrance, he saw two policemen coming out, with Philipp Mattauer between them. Mattauer's face was as sleek as always, but it didn't contain his usual merriment. It was grim and bleak. Even under these circumstances he was elegant; the policemen became a sort of honor guard in his presence. For just a second Mattauer and Navratil exchanged glances, and Navratil lowered his head ever so slightly – it was the equivalent of a deep bow, which no one saw except perhaps Mattauer. Then Navratil turned away, looking straight ahead down the street. And Mattauer was hustled into the police car.

All things considered, looking straight ahead down the street was the best thing he could do so that he wouldn't get thrown out of his office where he was still ensconced against all expectations. Looking straight ahead, especially when one of "them" came by, strutting erectly and challenging everyone with a glance. Leopold walked past them as if nothing was wrong, and they probably noticed that somebody had just passed them as if nothing was wrong, although something was wrong, and they gave him a sneering glance that he felt in the back of his neck. But frequently it was good to take a look around, too: a sinister animal would pop up, an eagle with wings spread, squatting atop a Swastika. When you saw it on a billboard, on a bulletin board or as the letterhead on stationary, you would be well advised to read exactly what was under it. It gave orders, restrictions and announcements, and if you read everything carefully and thought about it carefully you knew what was in store for yourself and for others. He could take care of himself or warn somebody else: "Watch out, put this or that in a safe place, or else..." and he could keep his position in the office as an indispensable jack-of-all-trades. Obviously there were also a great many changes in the office: a new director, as was to be expected; and new colleagues, rigid and with defiant expressions. But since they were all new to the office, they needed someone who knew his way around and knew everything. For Leopold it was a question of 'to be, or not to be' – as a former member of a dissolved Catholic fraternity, he could be thrown out on his ear at a moment's notice. But if he knew everything, from the most convoluted accounting regulation to the oldest Imperial code, then they asked him – he was allowed to explain, could look the questioner straight in the eye...and keep his job.

He rarely saw Rosi these days, and when he did see her, they talked at cross-purposes. But one evening Rosi called him at home: "Could you please drop by for just a minute or two?" Her voice made him tremble: never before had she played up to him. Neither of them had ever tried to forge the kind of bond Rosi was now offering him.

"Yes, I'll be right there."

It was clear to him that he was urgently expected. But he deliberately took his time, strolling through the glass entrance and up the stone steps, his eyes following the lines that an artisan had drawn in the plaster of the stairway. In front of every doorway the decorative lines separated into leaves, as they did in front of the nameplate with "Lemnitzer" on it. He pressed the doorbell.

"Come in!" He had been in their apartment many times before, but since the moment Rosi had self-consciously uttered this invitation, it was a different place. It wasn't the apartment that was open to him – it was Rosi herself. He entered.

"Would you join us for a cup of coffee?" Her father was sitting at the coffee table in the salon. When Leopold entered, her father stood up and offered his hand. "Hello, please sit down," he invited their guest. An easy chair in gleaming light brown wood enclosed Leopold with its armrests. "How are you?" Herr Lemnitzer continued. "Thank you for asking. These days no one's fine, but as far as I'm concerned, things could be worse." It wasn't necessary to ask about the host and hostess – he could spare them having to talk about it. "I still have my position in the office. They still need me for the time being."

Frau Lemnitzer brought in coffee and cake on a tray. "Hello. You can see that our maid Anna has the day off." She placed the tray on the table, Leopold rose and kissed her hand, they ate and drank. Rosi mentioned something about a performance of Schubert's *Unfinished Symphony* when they had eaten the same cake beforehand and which she always remembered when they had this kind of cake. Leopold remembered the part in *Struwwelpeter* where the dog sat at Friedrich's table eating cake. And lo and behold, four people – two old and two young – sat around a table and were as close as a family. But the tension he had first felt in Rosi's phone call grew with every word that didn't confront their true circumstances. When Frau Lemnitzer had passed the cake a second time, it came spilling out of Rosi:

"I haven't told you yet," she said loudly, "but we're leaving."

Leopold sat in silence, stunned.

"We're going to America and would like to ask you to help us."

"Yes, I'd be glad to. But I don't have any contacts with America."

"That's not necessary. We've got our visas and have paid our taxes. We've liquidated our estate, the remainder here will be picked up tomorrow by a moving company and put into storage. We don't know if we'll ever see any of it again. But we've packed a few things in two suitcases, rather valuable pieces that we've hidden away. And we're asking you to take them over the border to Tarvis and give them to a friend of ours at the train station. He'll forward them to us. You do go to Carinthia sometimes, don't you?"

"Yes, of course," Leopold responded, confused.

Rosi pointed to a corner of the room. "Do you see those two suitcases?" She went and got one, and Leopold helped her. She opened it for him; inside were a few suits, shirts, underwear, and three neckties. "This is travel luggage for you that anyone would find plausible. But there are other things in there that people can't see. Between the leather and the lining in the top we've hidden a few postage stamps; when we sell them, we can live off of them in America for a year. Under the lining in the bottom is where we've hidden the Dürer that used to hang over there on the wall; that will allow us to keep our heads above water for a second year. There are a few things in the shaving kit." She opened the kit, inside were a golden pocket watch and three diamond-studded tiepins. "Since you are a high-ranking traveler, these won't be out of place. And you are taking this pearl necklace to your Italian girlfriend." He wanted to ask if she had already found a girlfriend for him, but he suppressed the urge. Rosi continued to explain: in the second suitcase there were more postage stamps, an etching by Rubens, and two diamonds in a bar of soap. She closed the suitcase and looked him in the eye. Her devotion and her calculation converged in her purity of heart. If only she could feel and think this way about him...

"Fine," he said.

"Come now, eat another piece of pound cake with us," she invited him. He then learned that they would travel first to Philadelphia, and then they would decide what happened next. "Isn't our friend David Richardson there?" Yes, he was there. Maybe he was already waiting for Rosi.

"Would you like to take one last look around the house?" Rosi asked, when Leopold's plate and cup were empty. "Yes, I'd like that very much." Her mother smiled at them, her father went into his study. Rosi put her hand on the display case. "Look at this." On a coffee cup with a gold lip you could see a wooded valley, a creek flowing toward the viewer. A boy was lying on the bank, playing a flute. "He was always my secret boyfriend. Now he has to stay behind. But in reality he won't be here, only the coffee cup will remain here, I'll take him along so I'll recognize him again in case he's playing the flute along the banks of the Ohio River. And the dancing girl over there" – a small naked dancing girl in bronze was stretching her limbs – "that's the way I always wanted to look. Till now I haven't succeeded, maybe I'll be able to do it in America when we have to ration our food. At least I'll be able to take my childhood illusions along in her place."

"You're going to take along a little bit of everything?"

"Yes – or almost everything."

A bronze Valkyrie raised her sword, and in so doing exposed her breast. "Don't you want to leave her here?"

It took a while for her to find the right words: "Wagner was my idol, and in some ways he still is. He'll probably continue to be my idol in America, too."

"I'm sorry, but there's something I don't quite understand. Your ancestors came from the Promised Land and somehow arrived here to keep faith with their god. And you believe in Richard Wagner. And even more so now, when you and your family are being driven away, in one sense in Wagner's name."

"Yes, it won't be easy to break myself of that habit. But we also let ourselves be chased out of Egypt in Yahweh's name. Back then He showed us the way through the desert as a pillar of sand, and when people caught up with the pillar of sand, it blew sand in their eyes and ears."

"You're deeply religious. But if you allow Wagner to be an incarnation of God, why not Christ, too? His Sermon on the Mount is at least shorter than the *Walküre*." A park bench and chestnut trees shimmered through an age-old debate.

"How can you Christians insist that God came to earth as a man, as a rabbi with earlocks, no less?"

"God is wherever He wants to be. On the exodus from Egypt He led you as a pillar of sand – just ask Moses, he was there and wrote it all down."

"Now there's a picture for you: the Israelites saw the pillar of sand and believed they had to follow it, according to God's will. And since you can't see God, they just thought He was inside the pillar."

"Of course, first He was in the pillar, then in the tent of the covenant, and in the temple. And during the Babylonian Captivity the children of Israel finally discovered that He actually can be everywhere. And His word is everywhere as well."

"But Christ was not a word, he was a man."

"Every word must be understood in its situational context. You don't know what situational context is, only lawyers know what that means. Those are the circumstances in which a word is spoken and which give it its meaning. When you say 'Bismarck,' you mean a jelly-filled pastry, and when I say 'Bismarck,' I mean a world-famous politician – except when I'm talking with you. Then I'd rather be talking about pastry because I want to be on your wave length."

"That's why Christ is still a man. Our housekeeper also argues non-stop and she churns out situational contexts on an industrial scale."

"But she doesn't proclaim the word of God. Christ proclaimed the word and exemplified it throughout his life."

"You also seem to proclaim a lot."

"But I don't require a copyright. I simply quote it in my usual modesty."

"Aha!"

"Let me explain it to you in a different way: Once upon a time there was a Koran school, *Mu-atazila* or *Muta-azila*..."

"Why, what a wonderful knowledge of Arabic! How long have you known Arabic?"

"That's not an original idea, I got it from a Biblical scholar you've never heard of. These *Mu-tazilites* believed in the absolute Oneness of God and therefore concluded that the Koran – being God's word – must have been in God since all eternity, because otherwise there would have to have been some other divinity beside God, thus a kind of second God. And that's exactly the same thing John means when he says: 'In the beginning was the Word, and the Word was with God, and the Word was God.' So the Muslims and we believe the same thing, even if they call it the *absolute Oneness* and we call it the *Trinity*."

"And so we Jews are supposed to join the majority, since we are overruled?"

"That's not necessary, because every God – ours as well as yours – is threefold, because the mystery of the world is threefold. It consists of the mystery of creation, the mystery of the commandment which isn't logically justifiable, and the mystery of our conscience."

"Creation is eternal matter..."

"Matter isn't eternal, because it's in constant motion, and motion signifies time, and time isn't eternity..."

"Fine, whatever you say. But the commandment and our

conscience aren't mysteries at all. They are the result of natural processes."

"If you look at it that way, you misunderstand both of them. Even your Richard Wagner is the result of natural processes. But even if I understood them, that still doesn't help me understand his *Flying Dutchman* or even his *Parzival*. And while he was composing, he didn't give a tinker's damn about natural processes because he was concentrating on harmonics and on his infrequent ideas – that is, when he wasn't sitting on a triad for a hundred bars, like at the beginning of the *Rheingold*."

"But composing is nonetheless a natural process."

"Don't you understand? When a conductor studies the score of the *Rheingold*, he's interested in the sequence of notes and harmonies, not in the fertilization process by which little Richard was conceived, or the slap in the face he got from his father for pounding on the piano. And the conductor doesn't give a hoot how many times Wagner scratched his head while composing. Speaking of the sequence of notes: when you perceive a sequence of notes as a melody, that's the same irrational process as when you perceive the will of God in a Biblical commandment or in your conscience."

"So it seems as if there's a divine quadrumvirate – the Father, the Son, the Holy Ghost, and Richard Wagner?"

"Or should we add you to the group? You're so lovely that the outside world calls you 'the divine woman.' But creation, standards, and our conscience are vital necessities. If you don't know what is right and what is wrong, as a consistent relativist all you can do is just sit in Café Landtmann and drink a glass of water. Because as soon as you order even a small cup of coffee and the waiter asks you to pay, the question arises: should you pay your bill? And you can only judge that by means of principles and according to your conscience. You don't need Wagner to make up your mind."

"That is quite a clever argument. Did you make that up?"

"Some of it. I took an excellent course on the philosophy of law. The last class meeting took place on Himmelstrasse, the heavenly road."

"And back to Christ – if I slap your cheek, will you turn the other one?"

"For you? With pleasure! I'm a masochist!"

"And for Hitler?"

"Reluctantly. By the way, Hitler considers himself to be the executor of a natural law, so we have to show him that he can go jump in the lake with his natural law. Every rule has its exception."

"Hitler is no exception. He simply demonstrates that the rule is wrong. If you go along with something someone else does, then you are complicit in what he has started."

"But when you applaud Wagner, you're also complicit, because Hitler thinks that he himself is Wotan and believes you're applauding him – him and his divine guidance."

"That is no reason to consider Christ God…"

"If you think about what I've told you…"

"I will think about it in America."

"Think about it, but I'm afraid you won't think about it, you'll just keep arguing with me from a distance. All along I thought your God was Gainsborough. What do he and Wagner have in common?"

"Nothing. I love Gainsborough, and he used to peer over my shoulder when I drew. Through Wagner I glimpsed the depths of the world."

"The same depths in which his even more fervent admirers now want to hurl you."

"Yes, that probably makes it easier for me. You have to console yourself somehow. Let's look at the other things."

Polished glasses of various colors were on display, empty and irrelevant if someone didn't fill them with some type of beverage. And that had probably never happened with this glassware.

On a coffee service wild flowers bloomed in all the colors of the rainbow. "Chancellor Ignaz Seipel drank coffee with my father out of these very cups. During the currency stabilization he came to ask for my father's advice."

"Now our old stable schillings are gone, and Seipel along with them."

She inspected the bearded gentlemen and buttoned or unbuttoned ladies who were waiting to be admired in their gilded frames. "Those are my ancestors. I am taking along a photograph of each of them and one of myself. Every one was important. This one was a senator, that one was chairman of a museum association, and that one was also something or other. All of them were something or other. If these people seem a little peculiar to you, come and I will show you something else."

She led the way out into the hall and opened a door through which Leopold had never passed. A bed with a pink damask comforter and matching pink curtains reflected the blossoming of the girl who lived here. The glass doors of her wardrobe, also screened with pink curtains, concealed the feminine wiles with which Rosi had bewitched so many men. A bookcase contained all the knowledge about the secrets of the human soul: Schnitzler, Stendhal, Galsworthy, Dostoyevski, and others; nearby, a seating arrangement, featuring a sofa as a comfy spot to read. "This was me, here in my room."

"Yes, that was you, and is you."

"And all that will stay behind, except for a few items of clothing which I will take along."

Leopold picked up a small teddy bear which was sitting on the sofa and put it in his coat pocket: "Look, I'll take this along, and you can get it back from me later. I'll find a good home for him."

"Thank you." For the first time he saw the little girl in her smile. "And what of yours should I take along to America – I mean, from you personally?"

She stood there before him, the little girl, who as a grown-up young woman had wanted to argue with him about Christ and Wagner; he had served up tennis balls to this perky young lady and criticized her drawings, simply for the fun of criticizing. And she had chided him for being a philistine, for the fun of chiding him. And behind him stood Erika in her blue dirndl with white dots. "From me you can take what I will bring you later – the things in the suitcases. And the teddy bear. He will always stand by you, and sometimes he will remind you of me. But I do not want to send my ghost along." As they exchanged glances, the point of their separation was complete.

Father Lemnitzer was waiting in the foyer. Her mother emerged from the living room.

"Is there anyone who could report me if I sneak away with two suitcases? How do you get along with the housekeeper?"

"Not bad – but you never know," Frau Lemnitzer hesitated.

"It would be best if you invited her to come up and then offer her a parting gift – and while you're talking with her, I'll disappear out the door."

He went into the bathroom. The front door creaked and the housekeeper insisted: "But, madam, you really don't have to do that..." Then he shook hands and rushed away with the two suitcases.

As he reached the street and turned the next corner, he felt more at ease. He calmly walked along with his suitcases, but there was still something behind him, a vacuum that attracted him, an unsettled debt. The paving stones he traversed were rectangular, and it popped up from the rectangles – the final answer, the answer he had owed for years now:

Everything that someone puts in a man's head assumes the shape of his head, as wine in a wineglass intrinsically takes the shape of the glass. And when God takes the shape of the Trinity in someone's head, because someone comprehends Him in three aspects, then he really has it! – And that's my own idea!

He turned and glanced back over his shoulder, but it was too late. Let the dreamy boy on the Ohio River continue the debate with Rosi. The following weekend he took the suitcases to Tarvis and returned with a crate full of peaches.

One month later Leopold became engaged to Erika. When he kissed her, he was aware of nothing beyond her. But when her head rested on his chest, he gazed over her shoulder into an exciting New World. He had to venture forth in order to see her homeland and meet her relatives.

Late one afternoon they got off the train, grimy from travel. And in front of the station they found a local bus with a lion coat of arms violently shuddering on its radiator. The bus drove through fields, meadows, and flourishing front gardens, then through towns with their churches and country inns. "Tell me something about your homeland! In this village you went to your first local fair and went on a binge for the first time, and over there, in the gutter, was where you slept it off."

"No, I was never here for a local fair and never slept off a binge," she defended herself. He loved her most of all when she wore the expression of an offended mouse. They got off the bus in a charming village.

"My father is the principal of the local school," Erika said, and pointed to a school building painted yellow. They walked on past the building, turned down a side street, and strolled a while between orchards and flower gardens. Then Erika opened a garden gate and they approached a front door surrounded by larkspur and marigolds. "We're home!" Erika called out in the foyer, and her mother scurried from the kitchen, her father appeared from a room across the hall. "Well, hello, you two," her mother called, took Erika's face in her hands and gave her a kiss on both cheeks. She hesitated when she came to Leopold, and asked: "May I give you a little kiss, too?" And Leopold also got a kiss on each cheek. Erika's father had a high forehead and several red veins in his cheeks and nose. He shook hands with Leopold, led him into the parlor, and poured a clear fruit brandy into two tin cups. "Here's to your health!" he exclaimed, handed a cup to Leopold, and raised his own. Leopold emptied the cup, and her father refilled it.

"So, I'm getting a son-in-law from Vienna! How are things in Vienna? And how do you like it here in Carinthia?" "Thank you, I like Carinthia a great deal. But more than anything else, I like the most beautiful woman in Carinthia," and he put his arm around Erika.

The table was set, and her mother immediately served dinner. Leopold praised the wonderful meal and the beauty of Carinthia. "Yes, our province is certainly beautiful, but we've had to fight to retain it. Have you Viennese ever had to fight to retain your province?" her father challenged. Leopold countered: "After the war we also had to fight for our province – against the Hungarians, who wanted to take Burgenland away from us." Erika's father raised his glass and toasted Leopold. With that gesture he accepted Leopold into the family, as a man, as a worthy successor to the whisky-drinking old soldiers, and as his son-in-law.

Leopold and Erika were married two months later in the Rosegg parish church in the Rosental.

A year later Erika gave birth to a child. Not long after, the war broke out. It was such a pleasure to stroke the tiny head with your protective hand, even if you knew that you couldn't really protect it and that you yourself were in greater danger than the child – all around him young men were being stuffed into coarse green uniforms and carted off to kill and be killed. He couldn't be indispensable to his office forever. By now the new managers and colleagues knew their way around and wanted to fight on the home front rather than on the Eastern Front. Every day that he could spend at home with his wife and child was a day to the good, but a day full of anxiety, dreading that envelope with the imperial eagle and swastika on the outside and a duty assignment inside. And in the end it was almost a relief to have it in hand – his fear was conquered. Now he could worry about something else. The air war had begun, in the parks concrete monstrosities began to sprout – anti-aircraft towers. If you were considered good at calculations, you could be called to serve in the anti-aircraft batteries and even stay in your home province. When that happened, in these worst of times that was the best thing that could ever happen to you.

You know that whatever I said politically, I said openly, and whatever I did, I did openly. I can't imagine what I'm supposed to be hiding from you," Mattauer said. Behind his back someone raised a blackjack:

Uh! – That'll make some serious work for the dentist.

More work for the dentist.

One for my father – he's watching over me.

Father, be proud of me!

One for the Indian, Leatherstocking, on the martyr's stake –

One for Saint Sebastian –

"Uh!"

"Uh!"

"Uh!"

The last three were too much.

"If you really think you can hide something from us, you'd better think again. As for today... you're dismissed!"

Mattauer was turned around and led back to his cell by the two guards who held him up. In the cell there were five other detainees sitting on a bench. They squeezed closer together to make room for him.

On the opposite wall the outline of an upholstered sofa that was previously here was barely visible. Here a lovely blonde woman had once purred: "It's lovely to be in Vienna," had undone the ribbon on her negligee and sunk into the arms of a young man. The bed for the two of them had stood where the wooden bench now pressed against the welts from the blackjack.

Along the narrow wall of the room a mirror was suspended over a wash basin. When he turned and stuck his head out far enough, a familiar face stared back at him, but unshaven and pale with a filthy head of hair: Don't look, Christine, you don't want to see me looking like this. The man with the blackjack, in his polished boots, his riding breeches and his glassy eyes is much better looking. Some day, with nervous eyes he'll try to crawl off and hide from me in some dark alley. But for the time being, he is better looking than I am. Grillparzer always insisted: "The beautiful is good." He got that from the ancient Greeks. You think something is good when someone asks, "Why are you doing that?" and you're allowed to answer with "Just because," because no one dares question you further. The man with the blackjack dares to. A blockhead in polished boots barks at the world – the Minotaur in boots has become the measure of all things.

"Would you like one?" his neighbor on the bench asked and held out an open pack of cigarettes. "Thank you, very kind of you." The cigarette tasted good, especially when he was able to lean against the wall and not feel the welts on his back while he smoked.

"What did they want to know from you?" the cigarette donor asked.

"I don't know, they know everything anyway." Was the man who asked the question a police informer in their midst? He looked inconspicuous enough, medium height, medium blond, medium intelligence, with a face you forgot as soon as you looked away. Of course, everyone looks inconspicuous when the only thing he wants is to get off scot-free.

"They just want to teach us to behave ourselves in the future. To do that they're going to knock each one of us around again soundly, and then they'll let us go," claimed the hoarse voice of the tall fellow at the end of the bench. That guy was no informer. What he said didn't require a response, and it made sense. He was sitting there, stiff as a board, too stiff to bow before his new masters. He introduced himself as "Doctor Riedwanger," and the first thing that came to mind was a horse-drawn wagon, an old-time church square, and stacks of firewood. You couldn't help but notice him, because of his height, his integrity, and because it was a pleasure to calmly look him in the eye.

"We'll see what comes next," somebody else added, his name was Wallner or Waldner. Yes, we'll see. We'll see what's up and which way the wind is blowing, and then we'll choose whether we'll go along with the times or suffer more beatings.

Christine! My Christine! Can you hear me? They want to trample me, impale me on their horns, skin me and eat me. I've fallen among the beasts. You, my goddess, give me hope when I talk with you. I apologize. You are not a goddess, you are something better. Man creates his gods according to his own image – which is why there are so many gods that look like dogs, vultures, lions, cattle, and sheep. You will help me retain my humanity! I will always be proud of that kiss at the city gate and all the kisses that followed. I am proud to have walked down the staircase at the Opera Ball with you, your firm little hand in mine while they played the Fan Polonaise. With the same gold buttons that I wore on my dress shirt my grandfather had had an audience with the Emperor and presented him with a memorandum. Then he died in combat on the Isonzo. I really haven't had to make any comparable sacrifices, so I must be prepared for more if I want to be worthy of the gold buttons.

There he is, the great false idol, the blockhead goose-stepping around in polished boots, the by-product of the false idol of Providence and a civilization of sheep. I learned about his might in a small, bitter booklet. I opened it up one Sunday afternoon over apple strudel and coffee to spice up my afternoon snack – the ideas of Pascal: "One man says: 'How moderate he is!' and doesn't drink himself; the other man says: 'How much he can hold!' and drinks a similar amount." That man is powerful who only needs to get drunk, eat like a pig, or otherwise act like an animal...and be automatically in the right.

My beloved, brave Christine – we will hold our heads up high and look directly into the enemy's ignorant face. And some day, when I am on the outside again, we will defend ourselves, even though I don't know exactly how. But we will find allies, perhaps Dr. Riedwanger beside me on the bench who stands on his own two feet, when push comes to shove. Beside him sits Schremser, an engineer who is here, he says, because he was in the Marian Congregation. He has spoken some comforting words about Austria's immortality, the informer among us will have taken good notes, unless, of course, Schremser himself is the informer. The Social Democrat next to him, Zafranek, has probably still got a rifle buried in his cellar from his time in the *Schutzbund*, a Herr Pottinger insists that he was in the *Heimwehr*, God knows what he'll do in the future. Those of us here comprise a strange political wax museum, apparently someone is collecting us as showpieces of various political movements. But I won't stay a wax dummy, Christine, just as till now I've tried to show you that I'm not one.

The key turned in the lock, the door swung open, and a prisoner entered, shoving a pushcart with a tin tureen that smelled like potato goulash. A guard stood nearby, his machinepistol at the ready.

Zafranek expressed the obvious: "Potato goulash." Each of us retrieved his plate and got one ladle full with a piece of bread.

"It'd be even better with some sausage."

"And with fresh tomatoes and paprika."

"They're out of season right now. Maybe the Italians can send us some from Abyssinia."

A half-an-hour must have passed since lunch – no, only eleven minutes. Then ten more minutes – no, it was forty. It doesn't matter, dear Christine, whether time passes quickly or slowly; when I think of you, then time can pass as it wishes. If it doesn't pass at all, then I'll think about how, someday, the two of us will sit on the terrace of a coffee house on the Wörthersee and see a red-white-and-red flag flying from the church tower. Then I'll be the most blessed and most powerful man with the most beautiful woman beside me. And if I have to undergo interrogations and beatings until that day comes, I'm prepared!

A guard opened the door and hollered "Mattauer!" – Here we go to the next dozen beatings.

"You can leave," the interrogating officer said. Mattauer left.

The next day he went back to the office. His desk was empty. Leopold came to greet him, shook his hand, put his left hand on Mattauer's shoulder and said "Hello, Philipp!"

"Is someone waiting to use my desk?"

"No, but it would be best if you report back to the section head."

The section head thought it would be best if he had a meeting with the new personnel director, and the new personnel director said: "You are terminated for political unreliability." Mattauer went back to his office, shook hands with Leopold – "Goodbye" – and left the building that had become so hostile.

That evening he ran up the steps to Christine's apartment. "My God, Philipp, what did they do to you? I was so worried about you!" "Not worth talking about – not any more. Christine, we're going to get married as soon as possible, and then we'll move to my family's country estate!" "You're right, the two of us can handle it!" She was already out in the fields, standing firm, and beamed at him before she threw herself in his arms.

"That's just what I needed from you! I was always afraid that the cows in their stalls would just laugh at me the first time I turned up with a manure fork. But if you think I can do it, then it will work. The two of us will take charge!"

After the wedding they withdrew to the country estate. They moved into a corner room with a tiled stove, and sealed off the ballroom and drawing room. Next morning Christine grasped the broom with the comfortable feeling that only a broom can provide in a world full of filth. With the help of a hired hand, Philipp loaded the truck full of wood and drove it to a dealer. He hitched up the horses to the wagon for the fieldwork, and after the harvest drove the sugar beets in the truck to the factory. On the road he often encountered uncommunicative faces that seemed to express gratitude when he offered his "Good morning!" On the other hand, he also saw young men, trained to be goons, just waiting for the first opportunity to beat someone up. Sometimes he saw people who went about their jobs, watching for danger out of the corner of their eye, or subjugated boys and girls. There were many that you couldn't tell where they belonged. And old acquaintances who greeted him and meant "Are you still alive?" Afterwards he asked himself: Am I still alive? Or did I come here just to hide from the world? He sought contacts, even the most casual ones, and, whenever possible, he would shake hands with the workers in the sugar factory and was happy when they gave him a firm handshake.

Christine gave birth to two boys who were soon running after the chickens in the barnyard. In a checkered smock she loaded hay onto the wagon, shooed the geese out of the laundry room, and washed the family's clothes in the wash trough.

They weren't alone. On warm Sundays in springtime old friends began to show up at their farm, wearing heavy jackets and knickers, and, as it grew warmer, in Lederhosen and linen Alpine jackets. Willi von Johannstein came; he was even shorter than Christine. When he kissed her hand, he shrunk down to the size of a period, and then immediately expanded to an exclamation mark. "Do you know what Marschalek did, the bastard? He joined the army motor pool!" Sitting at the wooden table under the pear tree he told about Aslan, the actor, playing Wallenstein, and the wild applause from the audience in the sold-out Burgtheater when he said: "The Austrian has a fatherland and loves it, and also has reason to love it." He told about other friends: they drafted Hornik into the army; his wife was left behind with three kids... I see Urban once a month at the home of old Frau Perutz. She's quietly waiting to be deported and barely gets anything to eat from the government, so every month she hosts a soirée from what little she has; we all bring whatever we want to eat, and then she can live for awhile from the leftovers... Even Aslan was there once, and read things aloud you don't get to hear in other places... And a middle-school teacher named Frantischek, who looks the part, is now shoveling coal. He told us some things about the origin of the Austrian people in the early Middle Ages. He knew a great deal that I hadn't heard before..." And after exorbitant praise for the excellent peasant sandwich he said goodbye, and in so doing shrank from an exclamation mark back down to a period.

"What he said was quite interesting," Philipp later remarked to Christine as they were carrying the loaf of bread and the cider jug back into the house. "I remember a similar evening with the actor Aslan at the home of an old woman named Perutz; it may not have been Aslan himself... But a middle-school teacher who looks exactly the part, that's something new. You're supposed to shoot spitballs and paperwads at middle-school teachers, not invite them to soirées."

"Don't be such a snob. Middle-school teachers can conduct themselves very nicely. Besides, they know a great deal. And finally, some of your comrades in the Sturmscharen were middle-school teachers."

"Yes, they were all real good fellows, and I sat with them on our solidarity evenings. But Willi said it best: a middle-school teacher who looks the part. That means he looks like somebody who constantly wants to be brighter than anybody else and give out grades for your knowledge, your comportment, diligence, and appearance. Usually there is no place for someone like that at a party with Aslan. If that has changed, then the standard has changed. That certain something that used to make someone presentable is now something other than what it used to be."

"I can imagine many things are different than they used to be," Christine offered, and put the loaf of bread in the breadbox.

"And when I think about them sitting together, it makes me shudder. And at the same time I am consumed by envy because I am not involved. What is the common denominator?"

"That they aren't Nazis."

"Well, that's a lot. But Frau Perutz cannot simply invite everyone who isn't a Nazi to her parties. There must be something else besides."

"Yes, probably. Are you coming back out to carry in the rest of the dishes?"

"Be happy to. You see, that certain something is always the

composure with which one confronts his circumstances. In normal times the circumstances are social presentability and everything that gives someone this presentability – his intellect, his wit, his money, or whatever else he might be able to contribute. Our circumstance now is the dangerous position in which we are caught – Frau Perutz more than anyone else – and the certain something is the composure with which we face this danger. Willi and Frantischek are staring this danger right in the eye, and for that reason have become lords of society. And I wonder whether I still am, too. As the father of two boys, I am not eager to die. Believe me, our friends are cooking up something. Maybe they don't even know themselves what, but it bothers me that I'm not involved."

"Believe me, you have that certain something and are a lord in society, just as you've always been. Don't get so excited!"

On a Sunday afternoon not long after, Philipp's high school classmate Stefan Brandner strolled up to the castle just in time for a slice of bread and a mug of cider. As Christine returned to the kitchen, he leaned closer to Philipp and said somewhat more softly:

"I wanted to ask a favor of you, but at this point I don't want to concern your charming wife. Relatives of ours are harboring a 'submarine,' a fugitive – we call her Aunt Ella. I don't want to trouble you with further details – nowadays it's always better when you can say with conviction "I don't know anything about it." Day by day it's getting harder to provide for her. So then I was thinking: maybe you could contribute a little something from time to time, bread or butter or a few eggs, things like that. You travel around the area a lot. Possibly you might need to visit Dr. Pacher, the medical officer in Neulengbach, once a month. And while you're there, bring back a little something for Aunt Ella? It's a bit out of your way, but you could easily work it into your itinerary somehow."

A ray of sunshine broke through the clouds. Finally Philipp was once again a conspirator with his friends, and not merely the destination for someone or other's outing. Two days later, when Christine handed him the first package with a loaf of bread, a hunk of smoked meat – whether it was kosher or not – and ten eggs, she had become his co-conspirator.

The teacher and church organist Neumeister closed the lid of the organ console on which he had just been practicing an improvisation on themes from Schubert's German Mass. This evening it was still light outside, so he decided to take a circuitous way home, out into the countryside, across the creek toward the castle, and then return through wheat fields and beet fields. He paused at the creek by the wooden bridge – before him stood the broad wall of the castle grounds, dominated by chestnut trees. Between the treetops you could see the manor with the peeling yellow paint and the dingy man-sized windows. And as he approached, behind the lace curtain of one of these windows lurked the nose on the face of Mylord of and from Mattauer, pivoted once in a semi-circle to survey the land and his people, then turned back to his spouse's perfume and the aroma from a cup of bouillon. The teacher took three steps down to the creek, sat down on the bank, took a notebook out of his pocket and wrote:

> "The castle was built by the
> people's hand,
> Women and men laid the stone
> Which fueled the arrogance of
> the lord of the
>   land –
> Now the bastards celebrate
> alone."

Then he read the poem once more, crossed it out, thought a while, and wrote:

> "The people built the castle,
> Men, women, and children,
> Sweat on their brows, their backs bent,
> So the one inside could hold his head
> even higher.
> When will the people raise their heads and
> look
>   around,

Gazing up from the furrows of the fields?"

He put the notebook back in his pocket, left the creek to its murmur, the gnats to their humming, and the shadows to their lengthening. Then he took out the notebook again and wrote:

"O'er the fields the beaters drive the prey,
The lord of the manor fires his rifle – the
    wild boar falls.
Then the lord sits at table with his guest,
And, in the grass by the creek, the field-hand
    lays with the maid
And the common folk continue to shoot up
    like blades of grass on the bank.
Here we will lie, you and I,
Blossoms, fruit, and seeds we shall be,
And the grass shall sprout."

He reread what he had written two more times, then felt the wetness of the bank penetrating the seat of his pants, stood up, and went back into the village. He liked to pass by the schoolhouse because he enjoyed teaching. When he entered the classroom, the children stood at their desks, erect and silent. Then they listened and wrote what he had to say to them. And when they had been good, he would tell them about robber barons and other villains. He went home – his father was reading the paper in his checkered smoking jacket and his mother put their dinner on the table as soon as she heard him come in the front door.

After the meal he went to visit Gertraud Leibeseder, another teacher who taught at his school. Together they went for an evening walk. They liked each other. She didn't mind his eyeglasses and the blemishes on his face, because the face of an intellectual is endowed differently than the face of any average person. And she really enjoyed watching him strut at the head of the band. He liked her clear skin and her fine blond hair, even when she struggled to tame the loose strands. She was taller than he, and for that reason always stooped a bit forward – blond people are simply tall. It had grown dark, but out in the countryside on the field path he was able to half-read and half-recite his two poems. She smiled at the words "Here we will lie, you and I, blossoms, fruit, and seeds we shall be." But he, remembering the seat of his pants, didn't lead her down to that damp spot where he had written the word "here." He put the booklet back into his pocket and walked his girlfriend back home.

Before he went to bed, he sat down at the desk in his room and wrote in his notebook:

> "Look over the fields,
> Wade through the trees of the forest,
> You can see the twig sprouting before
> your very
>   eyes,
> The trunk rotting at your feet.
> Pluck the twig and discard the rot!"

And after a pause:

> "May doubt not divide thee now,
> May gloom not cleave thy bone,
> May grief not wrinkle thy brow,
> May pity not melt thy polished stone!"

In the last line he crossed out "pity not melt thy polished" and replaced it with "May the pity in thy breast not melt thy stone." Then he took a clean sheet of paper from the desk drawer, wrote at the top "Song to Humanity," and below that the poems he had created today. The next day he gave them to his father to read. His father read them twice, stared at the page, uncertain, and then said: "The title is a little…a little too overstated," and gave it back to him. His mother was standing by the hearth, watching the pots and pans. After dinner he went to see Gertraud and showed her his finished work, too. "Oh, you write so beautifully," she said.

Not long after, during the lunch break at school, the principal, Headmaster Prascher, approached him and requested that Neumeister come see him in his office after class. Headmaster Prascher was a party member, but didn't try to harm those who weren't. You were always glad to see him when he, lean and gray-haired, wearing gray knickers, pushed a wheelbarrow full of compost out to his garden or a load of vegetables in from his garden – at school everyone respected him. Neumeister, the teacher, entered. Headmaster Prascher offered him a chair, took an official piece of paper out of his desk drawer, placed it in front of him, and began: "Herr Neumeister, there's been a complaint about you, because you play organ in the church and because you marched at the front of the band during the Corpus Christi procession."

Neumeister perked up. Someone was playing a trick on him: "Playing organ is a part of my profession as a teacher and as a certified teacher in music. I must constantly practice music if I don't want to lose my craft. And as band director I cultivate German music extensively, I've already rehearsed eight German military marches and even composed a medley of German folk songs which will soon be performed by our band. And the fact that the band marches along in the procession is a long-established tradition."

"I know. Strictly speaking, everything you do is permitted. But you are a schoolteacher and are supposed to educate the children in a national frame of mind, not in some dubious churchly spirit. And you must present a commensurate image. I know you basically do that anyway, but you know where a good number of enemies of the German people have always stood and where they now, more than ever before, congregate. Everybody can see how the participants in the Corpus Christi procession cast defiant glances at the assembled National Socialists in a way they would never attempt under normal circumstances. And, as a teacher, you must distance yourself from all that."

Some dissonance needed to be resolved: "Headmaster Prascher, you yourself used to play organ in the church before you entrusted it to me. As an organist you cultivated German music and rendered a service to the German people. And I want to continue this service. If you'll only tell me who registered this complaint with you, I'll speak with him myself."

It was a civil servant in the district bureaucracy. Neumeister took a bus to see him. On the bus ride he toyed with his fingers, and as he saw the castle pass by in the distance, he clasped both hands together fiercely and rubbed them impatiently. When he arrived, he entered the office building and waited a while on a bench in the corridor. Posters of jubilant boys and girls with raised hands greeted him, and the mysterious shadow of the enemy, who is omnipresent and always listening, slinked past. Then he was called into an office. He entered like a dynamic organ prelude, raised his right arm in greeting, sat down, and began:

"Headmaster Prascher told me that there was a complaint registered against me because, as a teacher, I play the organ in the church and direct the band during the Corpus Christi procession."

"That's correct, there was a complaint about that."

"I would like to request that you allow me to continue doing so, because as a certified teacher of music I need this constant practice to remain competent in my field."

"Certainly, but as a teacher you offend people in those capacities. In this region the audience for which you play consists of almost all the enemies of the state, and precisely the Corpus Christi procession allows the Roman clergy and its adherents to inject themselves into the public eye."

"District Commissioner, you've come to us from Germany and will certainly appreciate that, of all things, music has never known a border between Germany and Austria. Besides, the people here insist on their folk music and their church music. So I beg you to allow me to continue in all my functions as a musician. However I am prepared to prove to you my loyalty to the Reich in a different manner, if you wish."

"How will you do that? You're not even a member of the Party."

"As a teacher I know all my pupils and thus have a reason to speak with their parents at any time. In this capacity I can find out nearly everything that takes place between the people in town and those in the district. Most likely I am the first person who would notice any kind of subversive conspiracy hostile to the state. In cases like that I can provide you with inside information."

The other man looked surprised: "Excellent, if you would just..."

"But to do that I must continue in all my duties, or else the people will become suspicious."

"Fine, I'll agree to a trial run – Heil Hitler!"
"Heil Hitler!"

Neumeister went to the door, came to attention once again, and left the room. As he exited the building, he leaped down the last three steps. And since there was no bus due at this hour, he ran across the plaza and down the main street, past the expansive villa that had belonged to a Jewish lawyer and where a loyal party member now resided. Just as he started to perspire from his fast-paced walk, he came to a brook. Along the bank a path forked in his direction. He left the road and walked down the path until he disappeared in the greenery of a forest meadow. When no one could see him, he marched on, goose-stepping, brimming over with the Badenweiler March, until a root on the path spoiled his cadence. He tore off his coat and tie, washed his face in the stream, shouldered his coat and continued on his way. The path meandered onto his estate. Unnoticed, he entered. All around him the green leaves were resplendent, life flowed in the brook and shone through the tree trunks and branches. A pheasant flew up – the pheasant was Mattauer's property to hunt. And then along came one of the underlings, one of the dispossessed, but he held his head up high to see who that all belonged to, in other words who would reconquer it. He had gotten to the Jewish villa too late, but someday he would have a chance to grab it when the property of the nobility was transferred to the state. In the meantime, he had to prepare himself. The path led out of the meadow across open fields. He looked out over the land. A noose stretched out to the horizon, and he could tighten it around whomever he pleased.

He came to a crossroad. Just a few hundred yards on the right it passed a rectangular farm that was located between fields and pear trees. The hay had just been brought in, so the gate was still open. One of the farmer's sons was in Neumeister's class at school, so, in passing, he could briefly talk about the boy's progress in school. He approached the barnyard, a dog barked at him, first from the front, then from behind him. He went through the gate and saw the farmer in rubber boots crossing the barnyard. "Hello, Herr Leitmayr," he called to the man. "I don't want to bother you, but since I was just passing by, I wanted to ask how your son Hans likes my class in school."

"Say, thanks for askin'. He'd better like it," the farmer answered and stomped over to Neumeister. "Somehow all of us learned a trade, and he'll have to learn a trade too."

"Are you hoping that he will take over the farm?"

"Yeah, could be. My older boy'd rather do somethin' else. He wants to be 'n engineer or somethin' like that. Nowadays they all want to go to the big city."

"You're right. Your neighbor over there in the castle did it the other way around. He came from the city to live out here. He likes it here. Do you think it's at all possible that a city fellow can run a farm?"

"Yeah, seems like he's got him some hired help, and he drives his truck or his horse-drawn wagon all over the place. Besides, this kind of work ain't all that complicated, so there's no danger of forgetting how to do it."

"Where all does he go in his truck, if he's so busy?"

"He'd be taking his sugar beets to the sugar factory and his wood to the sawmill. And he'd also have to drive to the farm bureau warehouse."

"Do you know him very well?"

"Well, we say 'hullo' when we see each other. He's always perty friendly."

It was better not to ask any more questions so the farmer wouldn't make a face and the dog begin to growl. "I hope I haven't kept you from your work too long. See you later!" That's the way to do it.

When the grain had been brought in and the sugar beet harvest taken to the refinery, Mattauer in his Lederhosen and loden coat went through the woods to mark trees that were to be cut down and also to estimate one last time the stock of small game for the hunt. The radio announced a straightening of the lines along the Eastern Front and requiem masses were being read in church for three farm boys who died as war heroes. Neumeister drove back to the district office. The noose was closed. Bit by bit he had tightened it: in conversations with plant managers who were glad to show their factories to his class; with the foreman of the sawmill who had a crucifix over his desk and had so many good things to say about the friendly Herr Mattauer who had also been a member of the gun club and had shot at painted targets with him until the club had been placed under the protective auspices of the state ("You know how it used to be..."); with the manager of the sugar factory sitting beneath the portrait of Hitler, who had exchanged some business talk with the lord of the manor; but also with the workers and the foreman, Mylord Mattauer had thawed out and shaken hands with everyone; with the warehouse administrator who wore the party badge, who had only signed receipts for Mattauer, and with the warehouse helper who had been in the Heimwehr home guard and had such huge paws that you couldn't even begin to get upset with him when he used his mitts to shake hands with Mattauer's delicate hands that were accustomed to fountain pens and champagne glasses: "Now there's a real gentleman!"

Neumeister, the teacher, was also a gentleman. That's why he didn't show any emotion. He spoke with all of them, was proper, businesslike, and polite. Proper, businesslike, and polite, Neumeister tightened the noose. Mattauer had taken part in the hunt club's Hubertus mass, and from there he, like Muhammad, had ascended briefly to heaven, but returned promptly to the roast Hubertus venison in caper sauce; you could see a shiny silver chamois waving above his Styrian hat. At Sunday mass he normally wore a massive golden halo, embossed with small, not too pretentious diamonds. He greeted Croatian road workers in Croatian – he would surely greet Stalin in Russian. With a French forced laborer from the stone quarry you could hear him making dignified noises through his nose, which was enough to make a good German sick to his stomach.

But the thing that counted most: "In our village we only have one truly interesting fellow, that would be the lord of the manor, Mattauer. He gets around on his many business trips and selects his contacts in such a way so that he can talk as long as possible with enemies of National Socialism."

"Yup, we're aware of that. That's always the way they do it."

"He's on good speaking terms with the manager of the sugar factory, Hausner, a former member of the home guard, and with the foreman of the saw mill, Weghuber, who's definitely not a National Socialist. In addition, he fraternizes with the workers in the sugar factory and in the warehouse, and there are most likely some Bolshevists in that lot."

"Well, those don't exactly add up to a smoking gun that needs to be pursued."

"No, not at all, but it could pay off if we keep an eye on them. I also find it interesting that Mattauer attends the evening chamber music concerts at the home of Dr. Wegrostek, a former functionary in the Patriotic Front. Some of the musicians are Court Counselor Kerbler and Reiter, the police captain who was forced into retirement."

"Chamber music isn't exactly a subversive activity."

"When these people are present, it certainly is. When you, as a consciously patriotic German, hear or play Beethoven, then you enjoy the music of the great German master whose genius conquered Vienna and strengthened the cultural unity between Germany and Austria. When Court Counselor Kerbler hears or plays Beethoven, he thinks he hears the composer who fled the musically devastated Germany for the dominant Vienna – I am speaking here deliberately from the standpoint of a Kerbler. When you hear the Emperor's Quartet, you hear the German national anthem, and your chest expands with pride. When men like Kerbler or Reiter hear the Emperor's Quartet, they hear the Austrian national anthem and they get tears in their eyes. And when a Mattauer hears the Emperor's Quartet, he dreams of the reestablishment of the Monarchy under Otto von Habsburg. You can even listen to Mozart as a great German master or as a Freemason who was blind to the conditions of his time and chose a Jewish baron as his child's godfather."

"Fine, that may be the way it is. But it's hard to see how this information will help us."

"Just take a close look at the guests who are going to participate in the hunt in November. And take a close look at the people from Vienna who visit him from time to time, then you'll know more. Yes, and one more thing: in the stone quarry there's a certain engineer named Schremser; he's the manager and also in charge of demolition. He's been sent there because he's 4-F and politically disaffected and has a detail of French laborers under him. He and Mattauer seem to have known each other from earlier times, both go to church on Sunday, and after Mass they once greeted each other like long lost friends. The way Schremser is classified now, he's no danger – he just provides paving stones for the Autobahn. But a politically disaffected man in charge of demolition with a detail of politically unreliable Frenchmen can possibly be dangerous."

"Hmm."

"And don't let me forget: every two or three weeks Mattauer drives to Neulengbach to a certain health official, a Doctor Pacher, who is also considered politically unreliable. I don't know what treatment Mattauer gets from Pacher, especially since he knows Dr. Wegrostek so well that he attends his musical soirées."

"Well, he's not on my beat any more, so my colleagues in Neulengbach will have to worry about it. Probably the one plays the violin better, and the other gives better enemas. And what you've been telling me is already pretty common knowledge. We know that there are enemies of the people out there, and that they like to hang out together. But we have to be careful to apprehend the right one."

"That's exactly why I've been alerting you to Mattauer. There are probably no charges against him on the books, but he was kicked out of his office because of political unreliability. And because of his contacts and his current activity he is by far the most mobile and capable of all those who could be considered enemies of the people. For that reason I recommend that you keep him under surveillance. And if at any time anything should happen that looks like subversive activities in the area, such as radio messages sent in code, such as laborers at the quarry deserting, or if any type of sabotage occurs, Mattauer is the only one who could coordinate isolated operations into one substantial activity."

"Fine, thanks a lot for your help."

Neumeister descended the stone steps at the gate with the stride of a lord of the manor. Then he went to the School for Continuing Vocational Education and requested information about a course on running a farm.

The foliage turned yellow and fell. In the fields hunters appeared and you could hear their shotguns ring out. Snow fell and began to melt again, Allied squadrons appeared on the horizon, rumors began to circulate, and again and again people would say about some young fellow or other from the area: "He died in combat." A police car stopped in front of the castle and took Philipp Mattauer away.

Private Navratil, as the direction finder, stood behind his anti-aircraft gun on the flak tower. Squadron after squadron of planes appeared on the horizon, bombs were raining down on all sides, and the city was being blown to bits. To his left, outside of his assigned area of fire, his parents' house – to his right, also out of his field of fire, the building where his apartment was and where Erika lived with his three-year-old daughter Mitzi. They must be sitting down in the cellar by now, which could collapse on their heads at any time. He couldn't protect them, or his parents either. He was protecting the apartment where the Mattauer family lived. Philipp wasn't living there at the moment, he was imprisoned in Dachau. Ever since the time he was arrested and released, he had worked on his mother's estate and in the end had been driving around in his truck. Probably someone thought that with all that driving he was a courier for some resistance group. Whether he was better or worse off than Erika and his little Mitzi in their ridiculous air raid shelter, at least he wasn't being bombed!

"Look straight ahead!" the Sergeant yelled at him. Behind him a string of bombs was just falling on his residential quarter – on Erika? He aimed his anti-aircraft gun at the middle plane in the squadron that was flying in, but before he could fire a shot, bombs were falling. His furtive shots didn't hit a thing. They couldn't have hit anything, because he was glancing to the left where a squadron was attacking his parents' house. Were they trying to kill his wife and child and parents? "Leave him to me!" he cried out, pulled the gun around and aimed it outside his field of fire, out over his parents' house. "Keep your field of fire!" the Sergeant shrieked at him. The squadron dropped its bombs and disappeared. Actually, he could have fired in any direction he chose – he didn't bother the bombers, and he didn't hit them either. He was low on ammunition and there wouldn't be any re-supply, because the front lines were inching closer every day and the Führer had more important things to do than to protect the civilian population. Hitler was already impatient for the day when his hated Vienna would finally look like Bremen or Hamburg, and when the flophouse where he had lived would finally be bombed so that no one could ever put up a commemorative plaque which would remind future generations of his years as a tramp. In one sense Private

Navratil had completed his military assignment: Mattauer's house was still standing – from here you could easily distinguish the intact windowpanes in Mattauer's apartment. The Department Head would once again sit down beside his porcelain Chinese figures, and soon his precious son would return as a hero. When the Thousand-Year Reich had been kicked in the pants for the last time, they would all sit behind these glass windows, while he, Navratil, was perhaps taking the crushed bodies of his wife and child to the cemetery in a pushcart. He could see them sitting there, with unwrinkled, contented faces, full of reasonable plans for their son's future. He couldn't hear what they were saying, but every word was well thought out and would have an impact. As a landowner, old man Mattauer would still take care of his estate. But soon he would again be an important man in the nation, because as a former consular academician the Department Head (ret.) probably knew Serbo-Croatian or Czech or some other language in which he could converse with the Russians. All that was an instantaneous revelation for Navratil: the window, and behind it the easy chairs and the arrogant faces. Something inside him snapped. With a jolt his whole body tensed. Now he had the window in the crosshairs of his gunsight!

Somebody shouted, "Hey, Navratil! You crazy?" Someone else yelled, "Take cover!" A whistling sound hurtled toward them, they were on the floor, a thunderous roar permeated everything. Navratil felt a sudden jolt of pain in his thigh, his ears were booming, and the thunder reverberated from the palpable darkness of the stairwell. He knew immediately: "I've been hit!" He propped himself up and looked around, saw blood, contorted faces, and shell fragments. Then he slumped on the floor and doubled up, shivering.

The people in the temporary aid station were glad to be rid of him – when he crawled off in a makeshift bandage, there was room and food for another patient. He half-ran and half-hobbled through the city until he spotted an empty space where his house used to be. Panting, he stood before a heap of ruins. Panting, he struggled in pain up the steps to the door of his parents' house. When it opened, Erika fell into his arms, and seconds later he saw his little Mitzi sleeping on his parents' bed. His mother hugged him, brought him some pajamas and his father's robe, then tea and a piece of bread.

That night his father sneaked into the house, his face gray, and hugged his son. Behind the boarded-up windows of his insurance company, all he could do was turn away grieving people, people whose losses could never be made good. Two days later, after a heavy bombing raid, some men carried him in on a stretcher, dead. Leopold wanted to wear his father's black suit to the funeral, but his mother felt that his father should be buried in it, so Leopold put on the dark gray suit that his father had left him. It was impossible to get a hearse, but the vegetable dealer next door agreed to take the casket to the cemetery on his horse-drawn cart, since he was trying to scrounge some things from the Simmering truck farms. So they sat beside the casket as it jounced over cobblestones and potholes. Leopold held his hand over the casket lid so it wouldn't fall off.

Sometime between midnight and dawn, when you've been hounded through a thousand fears by a power whose face constantly changes but is nevertheless well-known, and are finally flung down on a wooden pallet where you lie bathed in sweat and shivering from the cold, your head resting on your twisted and almost dislocated arm – that's when you're the loneliest. Even when you know that the other men surrounding your cot are confronting the same fears and freezing in the same cold cell, you can't help them at that moment and they can't help you. Christine is lying awake at home in bed, thinking about her husband, the father of her children, and perhaps she is praying for him. Yes, Christine, it's not certain that we will ever see each other again, but we have to hope unswervingly that we will. Don't cry, Christine, don't worry, try not to imagine what is happening to me here. In any event it is worse than you can imagine. Go to sleep, and I will also try to sleep a bit, and I can do that better when I imagine that you, too, are sleeping. Tomorrow I have to clean away more rubble from the bombing. I will be all right, I work out in the open, in public, so my guards will have to refrain from their pranks. And with every chunk of train station and with every hunk of factory that I hold in my hand I can congratulate the American airmen that they hit their targets so effectively. Often enough they ultimately hit houses full of innocent people. But I don't have to clean those away, my job is working on military transportation and armament plants.

When they beat me, I keep saying to myself: This is for Austria – For Austria – For God and Austria. The greatest temptation is to say it and spit in their faces. But that would mean death, and would be a sin. I must love my enemies, now or never – one day, when they're hanging from the gallows, it will be too late. For Austria – for the spirit of Austria – for Grillparzer who said that the path of the new culture goes from humanity to nationality to bestiality. For the Lord Nelson Mass. For the Jupiter Symphony. For the spirit that will once again recognize you beasts as human beings when you have once again become human, although the prospect is not good. Once someone has adored the blockhead in polished boots, it is not so easy to re-grow a human head. This spirit rejoices from within the Jupiter Symphony, it radiates God's praise from a single female voice in the

Nelson Mass, it flows from Beethoven's Archduke Trio, and it provides an immediate answer to Schubert's question "To whom should I turn?" Bruckner's modulations and interval leaps grapple toward realization of God. But you Nazis won't understand this spirit, even when your Führer alludes to Brucknerian melodies. The most clever of you get carried away with Hegel's ruminating balderdash and with Nietzsche's fraudulent sermons, and you will be craving this poison even if someone takes away your Minotaur. But perhaps someday a woman's hand will stroke you or a pair of child's eyes will look at you and awaken something within you, something that had died long ago – if it can still be awakened.

Now perhaps I can sleep for another hour, if my arm can stand it, so that I won't collapse tomorrow! Good night, Christine! We'll weather this in body and soul – now for sure: All our action and work be pious song of praise...

"All our action and work be pious song of praise!" Neumeister improvised a few more bars, as the priest and his altar boys stepped to the sacristy and the congregation shuffled toward the exit. He rested on the final chord, then closed the score and the lid of the console and climbed down the stairsteps from the organ loft. He intended to go straight home when a thickset man with glasses pushed his way over and clung to him: "Allow me to introduce myself. My name is Schremser. I am an engineer and would like to have a few words with you!" It sounded like he had something to say.

"Pleased to meet you. The name's Neumeister."

"I would like to ask you to step outside, perhaps we could take a short walk together – wherever you want to go, naturally. But the others do not need to hear what we have to say."

Schremser threaded his way between groups of people, some talking and some listening, across the church square toward a side street with Neumeister behind him. They continued on, into the side street, past windows and the sounds of dinner dishes to a spot where they were shielded by two wooden planks and screened by the tops of apple trees. Then, glancing up and down the side street, Schremser began:

"First of all, I would like to congratulate you on your outstanding achievements as an organist. You bring a spiritual and artistic lift to the community that is a great comfort to many people, especially in times like these. We can be proud – you won't mind if I use the name that has been officially invalidated – that the people here in Austria, in the midst of war, get to hear such wonderful sacred music. It must mean a lot to them to be transported once a week from their war worries and their everyday problems and be reminded of higher matters. And it is a blessing – even though, in essence, it is only natural that they experience this deliverance right here in church during Sunday mass."

"Thank you for your generous compliments. I enjoy playing the organ and also direct our brass band, because I believe that music has a great power over people."

"Exactly, and I can tell from the way you play that you are determined to exercise this power for the good of mankind."

"That is my humble wish."

Engineer Schremser tried a different tack. "I am an engineer, of course, and engineers often tend toward a mechanistic and materialistic view of things – as long as the machine works, it's good, regardless of what kind of work it does. But I also come from a devout family, thank God, and have had it instilled in me from when I was a little boy that technology must always serve a good purpose in order to be good, and that God is the measure of what is good. And I feel I detect in your playing that you want to lead people to God. Actually, I have been listening to you play every Sunday for the past six months. I have not missed a single Sunday mass yet."

"I am delighted that we share the same convictions."

"I work over in the quarry – as a jack-of-all-trades, so to speak – in charge of blasting and simultaneously, because I know French, as a kind of personnel manager for the French laborers."

A group of people approached them. Schremser waited until they had passed before he continued: "Even if I am not in the army, I still belong to it, for all practical purposes, because the stones which we quarry are used for military purposes, primarily for the Autobahn which is, after all, a strategic highway. In this capacity I am just a small cog in the war machinery. But I wonder whether this machinery will always be able to fulfill its obligation for the good of the nation."

"That's an interesting question."

"What do you mean?"

"I've never considered it quite that way."

"I would like to add that one can only speak of the 'good of the nation' with the greatest caution. And, in any case, I believe that the moment will come when we – the nation – will have to take our good into our own hands."

"Yes... that might be necessary."

"Soon after the upheaval I began to approach people who had no freedom of movement and provide them with spiritual solace and, naturally, also with material support. For example, people who, for good reason, could not risk going to church on Sunday, could not risk leaving their dwelling – you cannot really speak of an apartment, their circumstances are so pitiful – I have read to them from the Schott Mass-book and sung the German Mass with them. In this respect I consider myself your professional colleague. And in this regard there is so much work to be done that we will have to join forces and pool our strength."

Neumeister couldn't believe what he was hearing. "You want to form a resistance group?"

"Yes, so to speak. I see I don't have to beat around the bush with you. Just look at the front lines: the Russians are advancing on us inexorably. Sooner or later they will want to take Vienna. If you look at Vienna's location and the surrounding military force field – I am speaking here as a technician – then you will conclude that Vienna can best be taken in a classical pincer movement. The attackers will either know that themselves or they will automatically be diverted to the north through the Waldviertel and to the south through the Piesting valley and the Triesting valley. In that case they will be confronted with the necessity of consolidating the two spearheads west of Vienna in order to cut off reinforcements to the Germans. And the point where the northern and southern spearheads meet will be right here or a few kilometers to the east. And the Russians will have to dig in here, because the German army will naturally attack them from the west in order to protect Vienna's rear. In that case this area will be the scene of the last great battle of the Second World War. That would mean the complete destruction of industry, culture, and finally all life in this region of *Ostarrichi* – the ancient province of early Austria. In order to prevent this, we must obstruct or prevent the German counterattack from the west. That means that, above all, we must blow up the bridges to the west and fortify the terrain so that the counterattack will collapse to the west of us. To accomplish this I can provide a squad of well-trained demolition experts – my laborers, of course. However, except for them I have practically no acquaintances here. I briefly met the owner of the castle when we were both in Gestapo custody, but he is now in a concentration camp. And so I turn to you with the question of whether you want to support me in this venture. You could take over the political organization, I could offer my services as a quasi commanding officer. As you can see, I have invested a great deal of time and thought on the military situation."

"Do your people know about your plans?"

"No, but I have made a list of the ones who would be interested – it's the majority of them. By the way, the list is completely innocuous – at first glance, it looks like a simple pay sheet. But it suffices when the head knows what it has to do, and then the arms and legs will follow."

Sieg heil and alleluia! This was just the man he needed! Neumeister's plan, staged with the eye of an artist, has paid off. By being who he was, he had laid the bait, and the fish had bitten. But Schremser by himself was a small fry who had little market value. If he reported Schremser now, he would have denounced a crackpot, and they already knew he was an enemy of the people. They wouldn't find any evidence, it was all cleverly disguised. Certainly Schremser was also clever enough to send him, Neumeister, on a wild goose chase so that he might possibly commit suicide by running straight into the arms of an informer – it was good that he, Neumeister, was himself an informer. Before he could make something good out of this deal, something good had to happen. The next couple of months would tell what and how. So waiting would be the best course of action. If he could offer the Gestapo an entire band of saboteurs on a platter, along with the corroborating evidence, that would show what he could do.

For lunch he ate the chicken noodle soup and steak that his mother had conjured up, and walked with Gertraud to the movies and then back again. All the while something was gnawing at his stomach, possibly the certainty with which the crazy engineer had predicted coming events and had formulated his plan. What if the engineer was not crazy at all, just remarkably cunning?

From Gertraud's house he went to have a beer in the Golden Lion. He often sat here in the evenings and eavesdropped: here in the inn he could learn what was up. He sat down at a corner table and ordered a mug of beer. A tall, gaunt soldier was just sitting down at a nearby table, exhaling a cloud of cigarette smoke and raising a mug of cider to his lips. Another soldier entered, approached the first soldier and asked: "Do you mind if I join you?"

"Please do, Lieutenant Colonel," the first soldier replied, and stood up.

"As you were. We're not on duty. My name's Hufschmidt. I've got a master's degree and am an army pharmacist."

"Pleased to meet you, I am Dr. Riedwanger, Private and Company Clerk, presently returning to my unit from furlough. My bus will be arriving outside any minute now."

"Well, let's forget about the Lieutenant Colonel and the Private, and speak man to man, or comrade to comrade, or if you prefer, from college graduate to college graduate. I think it's much more important — also for the outcome of the war — for soldiers to be able to communicate with each other on human terms too. The closer individual soldiers stick together, the better they will fight as a unit."

"Certainly, sir, if you ignore the fact that the two of us don't fight much as a result of our assigned duties."

"Fine — ignoring that fact. But nevertheless we are both soldiers and comrades. What's your opinion of the present situation?"

The tall soldier laughed: "My dear Herr Pharmacist, up till now no one has ever asked me what I thought of the situation or how I would conduct this war; as Company Clerk I have modest responsibilities. So I formally request to be excused from any duties on the General Staff."

The officer rested his elbows on the table and leaned over: "But we're both academicians, and so we both ought to have an opinion on what's happening. Besides, the war has just entered a very interesting phase. For example, just think about the recent offensive in the Ardennes…"

The private inhaled, snorting, then he drained his glass of cider, washing down everything that had been sticking in his craw, slammed the mug down on the tabletop, and cut loose: "Herr Pharmacist, if you want to know — the war was lost before it even began. And this offensive is a joke."

The Lieutenant Colonel looked at the Private, speechless. Then he pounded his fist on the table and exploded: "Well, I won't stand for talk like that!" He stood up and hurried to the innkeeper at the bar: "Did you hear what he said?"

"What was I supposed to have heard? I didn't hear a thing," the innkeeper answered. The officer looked around: the customers who had just been staring at him now looked away.

"So, that's the way it is around here. I'm going to report this to the mayor. Who's the mayor here?"

"That would be Reidinger, the druggist, up above the square."

"All right, thank you." The officer placed a Reichsmark bill on the bar and went out. As soon as he had left, the private pulled his legs out from under the table, stood up, towering like a church steeple, paid, and left the inn with a few unhurried giant strides.

Neumeister looked around — he was all alone. He had bet on the wrong horse. The hushed muttering from the other patrons about the militant troublemaker and their hushed agreement with the private's grim prophesy told him all he needed to know. Up to this point no one knew that he had bet on the wrong horse. Up to this point he could dismount without anyone noticing, but he wouldn't have much time. He paid and left.

Meanwhile the Lieutenant Colonel-pharmacist was knocking on the door of the mayor-druggist who invited him into his living room. The officer began: "I have to tell you about an extremely bizarre incident that just took place in the inn down the street…" and he told his story. "The thing that amazed me the most was the innkeeper's attitude and that of the other patrons. No one claimed to have heard anything, even though they certainly couldn't have missed it. The private didn't even make an effort to lower his voice. Does everyone around here share his opinion?"

The mayor inhaled and exhaled and inhaled the question one more time: "Yes. If you want me to tell you the truth, that is the thinking around here – at least the thinking of a great many people."

"But I don't understand. They are just wholesome farmers, not cynical, sickly city folk!"

The mayor leaned over the tabletop. "You and I are in some ways colleagues, I'm a druggist, so I understand something about chemistry as you do. Obviously, you understand more about it than I do. But I've been thinking a lot about the natural laws of a nation. And I became a National Socialist because I saw that noble elements remain pure and do not combine with other elements, while base elements make compounds with others. And it is the same with nations: the noble ones keep their race pure, and the nobler they are, the purer they keep themselves. I've always said that our nation must be pure gold. But the individual molecule doesn't know that, it acts according to its own laws, without knowing them – providence determines that. And it is the very same thing with the rural population: the people here are pure, wholesome Bavarians – especially the farmers – but they have not yet entirely understood National Socialism, even though it exists for their own good."

"That surprises me, in light of how much National Socialism has done for the esteem of the farming community."

The mayor rubbed his chin. "Yes. You see, the farmers aren't as concerned about their honor as about their money. And that the war would cost money was clear from the beginning." It felt good to stay calm when your brain was "at ease." Again the hostile gaze of the Lieutenant Colonel called out "at ease," but he was staring out into empty space: "You know the old proverb, 'Do you want guns or butter?' The farmers just want to sell their butter. And the rest of the people in town think the same, even if they aren't farmers."

"Is that everything?"

What did he mean, 'everything'? No, it wasn't everything, there was still more that could be said, but the mayor would have to consider carefully what he should say. He had gotten a half-truth off his chest, and now he felt more relaxed; one hand rested in his pants pocket, while the other man raised his in salute to the flag. He had articulated the simpler half of the truth, but he would have to think about the more difficult part. But, what do you know: this way he could prove that he was a human being and not some little cog in a flywheel: "No, there's still more..."

That was enough for the time being.

"All right – let's leave it at that. Good bye!" The officer stood up and left the room. The mayor opened the front door for him and closed it after him. The door was closed, and the officer noticed something else: it was locked. The officer stared at the locked door, then went to his quarters and fell into bed, still fully dressed in his uniform.

"They've taken him away," Christine had sobbed into the telephone.

"Hold on, we're coming," answered her father-in-law, the retired Department Head, Ferdinand Mattauer.

The next day a taxi stopped in front of the castle and Frau Valerie Mattauer got out, marched up to the front door, thereby reclaiming the land of her ancestors with each stride. After a kiss and a hug for Christine and the two boys she moved into her room, then she went into the kitchen and tied on an apron. Christine wasn't needed here anymore and went to get the broom to sweep out the barn. Two days later the old gentleman arrived. "Be calm, God will take care of things," he said as he kissed Christine on the forehead. The following day he was shown around the estate by Burgl and Mitzi, the only two servants who hadn't been conscripted into the military; afterwards he pulled on his rubber boots and hitched the horses to the plow.

At first the plowshare scratched over the ground. When you put your weight to the handles, it dug into the soil, would bounce off a rock, and pull to one side. But the farm horses knew their way around, and manual skills he had acquired years ago, partly for the fun of it, returned. The plow brought up row after row of fragile black crowns from the underworld. The bodies to which they had belonged filled the field, up and down the rows, jumbled and entangled, and grass, beets, and grain grew out of them. Romans had lived here, had formulated and circulated laws on wax tablets, had created an empire and let it degenerate. But whoever had a good piece of land stayed put, with or without the Roman Empire. Goths, Eruli, and Lombards passed through, and people said to them: "Please, help yourselves, that's all that we have" – after they had hidden sufficient earthen crocks of oil and grain under the floorboards. And the newcomers took whatever they could eat or carry off, raped the wife and daughter, and moved on. Some spread out over the countryside and stayed. And at the point when the daughter had a child, you made peace with the violent suitor – after all, you lived on in this child, and not every man was granted such a fate. The blisters on my fingers will soon break open. Plowing was a lot more fun thirty years ago, when I was still trying to impress Valerie. My poor boy, I'm ashamed of myself. I complain, and you are trying to survive things much worse.

And on top of it all the wind is blowing through your prisoner's shirt, and if you make a peep, someone will shoot you dead. When you were a small boy I once spanked you with my riding crop because you smeared the wallpaper with chocolate. I should have given you another piece of chocolate as a reward for the beautiful painting. But I always refrained from giving you too much chocolate so that you wouldn't have bad teeth. Now it doesn't matter whether you're buried with good teeth or bad. Oh, no, you're still alive, and your good teeth will come in handy. Oh, God, where is Your justice! And all this time I've been Your sheltered child: the Haginer family across the road has lost three sons on the Eastern Front, another one is missing in action. At least I can hope that my boy is still alive. When somebody has lived as long as I have and can only plow according to pre-drawn rows, hoping that he'll be relieved one day, he can be content with his fate and submit to divine providence. But woe to the people on whom a raving-mad butcher fulfills the divine plan which his Führer has set forth for him; the butcher bravely resists his inner temptation, refusing to bite when someone yells: "No, please don't bite!" while Providence says: "Oh, yes, bite!" But watch out, you brave butchers, many an inner temptation can't be suppressed in the long run. It can come to pass that suddenly God stands before you as inner temptation, so that you have the chance to hit him in the face. "Why are you hitting me?" He will ask, and you won't have an answer. Then you'll be silent and stare at the earth where someday we all will lie.

"Grandfather, we've come to visit you!"

Yes, come, you precious little boys, there is enough room down in the cellar for all of us.

Two separate thunderous roars shook the glass panes in the cellar window: the ones in the distance came from Russian tanks, the others from anti-tank guns on the ridge behind the village. The house was not in the line of fire. Besides, it could withstand several direct hits without collapsing, and if it did collapse, the cellar arches would still bear up. It could get serious if one of the two groups decided to take cover in the house. But the family could survive that, too. Death was all around, you just had to duck under his empty hand. Up above, a machine gun was now chattering. A burst of gunfire broke out, quickly followed by an explosion. Where was the anti-tank gun? It was gone.

"The shooting has let up, they'll be coming now. I'm going up to scout around." He had a white handkerchief in his pocket, on hand at a moment's notice. He climbed the cellar steps, dodged behind a door jam, and peered out. Russian tanks had advanced on the village. He saw only one, but there had to be several more. At the corners of buildings on the outskirts of town infantry soldiers had taken up positions. Two bodies were lying in the field. More Russian infantry advanced in a broad semi-circle. He took a step away from the door so that he could wave to them with his white handkerchief – and leaped back! Two SS-men were just coming around the corner of the garden wall, and behind them two Hitler Youths with a machine gun and a box of ammunition. One of the men pointed to a crater: "Set up here. The attacking enemy must be wiped out." And by the time the boys set up their machine gun, the SS-men were gone. The old gentleman stepped out from the doorway, took a quick look at the situation, then called to the boys: "Stop! There won't be any shooting around here! Throw that piece of junk in the creek, quickly, and I'll give you something decent to wear instead of those uniforms!" And when they hesitated, uncomprehending: "Are you crazy? Do you want to get yourselves and all the rest of us shot? Quickly!" The boys ran into the house. "Give them something to wear!" And now the moment had come: "Valerie, the flag! And the cider jug, a loaf of bread and some salt. They're coming!" Christine came running with the sheet, he hoisted it over the doorway. His wife carried a cup with a jug of cider, a loaf of sliced rye bread, and a salt shaker. At the same time a pole was shoved out of a window in the church steeple, and a white flag was unfurled. A shot rang out behind them, and the window facing the retreating SS-men shattered. At that point the war was over. A line of Russian infantry advanced toward the castle, the old gentleman waved his white handkerchief and called out: "*Zdravstvuite!* – Greetings, comrades!" The formation dissolved, the soldiers approached with their weapons lowered so that they could be welcomed by the master of the castle and drink some of his cider. The old woman had to fetch a second jug, and the two Hitler Youths, now dressed in baggy pants and shirts, each brought two more. From the village the electrician Klement and the innkeeper Zeller came running and hollered: "Herr Department Head, you can talk with the Russians, please help us!" The old gentleman could only speak a bit of Russian, so he clapped an officer on the shoulder and said in German: "You are a man of honor, I can depend on you!" and went with the two men back to the village. There, on the church square, people had already begun to crawl out of their hiding places and gather together. A high-ranking Russian officer called out: "You, to quarters!" The old gentleman went over to him, greeted him, and added: "*Vsevo khoroshevo.* – All the best." Then he tried to explain that everyone in the village was their friend and was prepared to help the Russians – he couldn't think of anything else to say. The officer gave some orders, and as the old gentleman turned to go back home, the officer called to him: "You mayor!" Nevertheless, the old gentleman went as quickly as possible back to the castle where his wife was ordering around a dozen Russians and assigning them to their rooms. Christine crossed the barnyard carrying a bag in one hand, a rock in the other. She had come up with this weapon some time ago. Out of the corner of her eye she saw a soldier standing under an archway, staring at her: "You German whore, belong now to me!"

"I am not a German whore, and I belong to my husband."

"You husband try kill me and me family."

"My husband did not try to kill you, but I will beat your skull to a pulp if you bother me."

"You Germans ruin our youths and our wives, what else can we do?"

"You still have your whole life in front of you and will find a respectable Russian girl."

The soldier turned and walked away.

The next day a youngish-looking man in glasses rang the doorbell and asked to speak with the mayor. Christine sent him out into the fields where the old gentleman was in the process of unloading manure. The man introduced himself as Schremser, an engineer and leader of the local resistance movement, and asked the mayor to say a few words at the funeral of a comrade from the resistance. That would be the teacher and organist Neumeister, who had struck up the white flag on the church steeple and been killed by the last shot fired by the retreating German soldiers. The engineer Schremser told a few more things about the resistance group of French laborers, who had, however, fled the battlefield before he could brief them on their mission. The old gentleman listened, without wanting to go into detail. He wanted to ask if his son had been involved, but he let it go – for the time being, it was all over. But the next day he went to the cemetery where the body was laid out and the mourners had assembled. The brass band, whose ranks had been thinned by the war years, played a funeral march, the procession approached the grave. There the old gentleman spoke a few sentences about the victims of the criminal state and of the senseless war. Suddenly he saw his son in the casket and was overcome with choking. But he wiped away the tears and rejected the apparition. The band played the song about the good comrade and the casket disappeared into the grave.

Several weeks later Christine was working in the vegetable garden. At one point she looked up from her work and saw a tramp in baggy clothing trudging up to the house. She recognized him, ran to him and threw herself in his arms, sobbing.

Engelhofer was sitting on a wooden bench in a bare room. On his right sat an elderly gentleman in a gray pinstriped suit. Engelhofer knew him from the days when he wore a brown uniform. The suit concealed his belly and his skinny legs. On his left sat two men who were also several years older than he was. Across from him there was now a lighter spot of dirty-gray paint on the wall – that's where the portrait of Hitler had hung until just a short time ago. The floor had been waxed long ago, there was dust in the corners. When he tried to relax, he bumped against one of his neighbors.

"What are they going to do with us now?" he asked, after an extended silence.

"The same thing we did with them," his neighbor on the right answered.

"What did we do with them?" Engelhofer asked.

"You know damn-well what we did with them," the other man said, and after a pause: "When the Commies get together with the clergy, between them they'll come up with something."

The neighbor on his left wheezed once briefly, arched his back, and then said: "The clergy aren't dangerous, you just have to go to the priest and have him certify that you've always been a good little boy. He'll give you the certificate on the spot."

"That won't work, I denounced our priest to the Gestapo," interjected the neighbor on the right.

"That doesn't matter, there's an order from the Pope that they've got to cover for us. He's already figured out that he needs us to fight against the Rooskies. Besides, they've got to forgive us, that's their job. Love your enemy – we were their enemies, weren't we? Well, there you are. Anyhow, not everybody's enemy, but enough."

They stared at the wall with the rectangle of lighter-colored paint. After a while, a policeman opened the door and called into the room: "Street cleaning detail, form up outside!"

"Do you mean us?" Engelhofer asked.

"You bet I mean you," the policeman answered. "Pick up a shovel over there and form two lines down in the courtyard!"

They stepped out into the corridor. Men just like them were coming out of other doors. Two Communist policemen pointed the way to a third man who gave each of them a shovel. "That's for you!" he said to Engelhofer, and gave him a pickaxe.

"Shoulder arms, forward march!" commanded the Communist policeman who had fetched them from the room. He marched at the head of the column, behind him twenty men with shovels and picks, bringing up the rear were the other two policemen with their hands resting on their gun holsters. The windows of the houses along the street were taped up with paper, the walls had bullet holes in them. Every so often the row of houses was broken by bomb craters and piles of rubble. They turned down the Wiedner Hauptstrasse – some branches of the boulevard trees had been cut down for firewood – and they marched on past the Chimneysweep Church that stood in the middle of the street, unscathed. Beside it a pile of rubble blocked the road. "All right, let's start right here," one of the policemen announced. "Dig out the streetcar tracks. Put the debris up there!" He pointed to the top of a mountain of rubble that had once been someone's house.

With his pick Engelhofer took a swing at the nearest chunk of wall. A wooden beam that stuck up out of the rubble was in his way. "Wood goes over there!" the Communist police officer ordered. Engelhofer and three others put down their tools and grappled with the beam until they could pull it out of the debris. "Put it over there!" the policeman ordered a second time, and they lugged the beam along the gutter to the front of the nearest undamaged house.

Engelhofer went back to hacking at the chunks of wall until he had separated them into individual bricks and mortar debris. Then he swung a couple of times aimlessly into the rubble because that was easier. Wood splintered under the pick. He groped in the debris and pulled out the leg of a chair, full of embossments and grooves. Lathe work from grandmother's time. He pitched it beside the wooden beam, then he unearthed three more wrecked pieces of debris and a seat cushion of pressed leather. He tossed everything over with the rest of the wood, to be used later by the Communist policemen for heating. "In any case, we're rid of this junk," he grumbled as he worked.

Two women in scarves and ragged loden coats approached. They stared at the pile of rubble and the men at work, and then tried to climb the mound. They began to search among the ruins for something salvageable. A policeman looked up at them, considering if and how he should officially respond, but then he simply turned away. "Do you need firewood?" Engelhofer asked. One of the two women looked at him, speechless, turned her back on him and kept searching. Engelhofer returned to hacking in the rubble and cleared away a squashed gas stove, then a twisted gas pipe. He turned to the policeman: "Scrap metal...?" The policeman pointed to the very top of the mound of debris.

Five men in ragged pants and jackets, noticeably more shabbily clothed than Engelhofer and his comrades, suddenly appeared and also began to shovel the streetcar tracks free of debris. "Where'd you guys come from?" Engelhofer asked one of them. "Where are we supposed to come from?" one of them growled back. "I mean, were you also roped into doing this?" "Nobody roped us in, we get five schillings a day and warm soup at night for clearing out this mess," the other fellow responded to Engelhofer's bootlicking. He sounded like a damn Socialist. Engelhofer despised the paper Russian schillings, but it was always better to have some than none. And, more than anything else, that man got warm soup with Russian peas, exactly what Engelhofer wanted most. Even if the man had rebuffed Engelhofer, at least they shared a common hunger. After a while, Engelhofer asked: "You guys Socialists?" "Yeah, now that we're allowed to be Socialists again," the other retorted. Engelhofer paused: at this moment he had found a link to this new society – by bootlicking, he was having a conversation with a Socialist who was just as hungry as he was. He kept on burrowing through the rubble, heaved the ruins of a window frame onto the woodpile, and let the Socialists see that he knew how to work. Planks from a bookcase ended up on the woodpile, right where they belonged, the books that gradually emerged from the debris he left to the men with the shovels. He uncovered a plaster arm from a pretentious torso that used to support a door or window frame, and heaved it way up on top of the pile of rubble.

Toward evening a truck rattled up, a truck that had been too wretched for the Russian to requisition. Engelhofer and the other men clearing debris loaded as much of the firewood as they had room for. Then they shouldered their shovels and picks, and under the watchful eyes of the policemen the clean-up detail marched to get their pea soup. The next morning they marched off again. This time it seemed easier to Engelhofer, somehow he felt...exhilarated. Maybe he was attracted by the plaster royal-and-imperial Rothschild Hercules that he was about to dig up and decimate. And the Socialists were back again, too. As he was clearing, he pointed to an old-Matzleinsdorf shanty with crumbling plaster and a corridor toilet that was probably clogged: "The Americans could have bombed that to smithereens, along with everything else." And when the man he was speaking to didn't answer: "Now you fellows will have to build something decent here, if the Commies will let you. It's your turn now."

That evening, as they were marching to get their pea soup, past the Chimneysweep Church which still blocked the middle of the street, Engelhofer mentioned to his neighbor: "If we shoveled hard enough, we could bury that church in rubble."

"The Chimneysweep Church," the man added, lecturing in an amused tone.

"Why is it called the Chimneysweep Church?" Engelhofer asked.

"'Cause it's got a chimney."

"Where do you see a chimney?"

"Who cares."

Hitler, Engelhofer thought. Hitler could have put a decent road there without a church standing in the middle of the street. Well, it's the Socialists' turn now.

The next morning he shouldered his pickaxe and marched off in the general direction of the Chimneysweep Church.

The last shots had been fired not so very long ago, people still recoiled when a door slammed somewhere in the house. Then a letter arrived, an invitation to the first official meeting of the *Vogelweide* fraternity since the war. It was signed by fraternal brother Fips, better known to his middle-class neighbors as Dr. Newerkla. The occasion was a wake in honor of fraternity brothers who had died in the war and in concentration camps – it was to be held at an inn in the seventh district that had been spared during the bombing. You made your way to the inn between mountains of rubble and bomb craters, sometimes you saw a familiar figure groping his way over rocks toward the same destination. Then there was a joyful shout, a heartfelt handshake and a goodhearted laugh that the two greeters were still alive. In the inn's spare room more familiar faces, emaciated and wearing tattered shirt collars, laughed at the sight of you. Some were missing, among them Ulrich Hornik. As a soldier with a radio on his back, he had absent-mindedly stepped on a landmine. Suddenly someone began to clap, others clapped along, and everyone looked over to the door – Philipp Mattauer, the hero of Dachau, was making his entrance, clutching a case of beer. The beer must have come from his family's private stock.

Dr. Newerkla, the last Worthy Grand Philistine elected before the war, held the address in honor of the deceased. The others listened, standing. After this official part of the program everyone sat down, and each asked his neighbor: "And what are you doing now?" Leopold heard Mattauer say "I'm going to…", and he listened closely. Mattauer already had a good position in the department of the ministry that dealt with the same affairs he had handled before the war. As a victim of political persecution, through his valuable contacts, and, not least of all, because of his abilities, he was the obvious choice from the outset to be the future Department Head. For Leopold Navratil that was a good reason not to seek a transfer into that ministry. Based on his professional experience, he should have been in the same department as Mattauer, but he wasn't in the same league, at least as far as political persecution. On the other hand, several National Socialists had been thrown out of Leopold's office. He could take over from one of them with good prospects for the position of director, in addition to the title and salary of a Court

Counselor. No one could begrudge him all that – after all, he had thwarted many of the Nazi rulers' infamous acts, or, when he couldn't stop them, at least warned the concerned parties; in his desk drawer lay several deeply moving letters of gratitude from emigrants overseas, among them one from Rosi Lemnitzer. He was happy that at such a great distance she had come to grips with her erstwhile relationship with him. Somehow she had realized that when all was said and done, the two of them belonged to different worlds – and for precisely that reason he was able to do something for her. In general, he liked his professional prospects: "At the frontlines you have to be brave, but not in the General Staff," he said, and by that he meant *frontlines* to be the lower bureaucracy, while *General Staff* was the ministry. Secretly he also wanted the title of Court Counselor, which, with the disappearance of the Imperial Court, had found refuge within the lower bureaucracy.

His hopes were not in vain – he soon became the deputy director of his office. Of course in that role he wasn't always as happy as he had hoped. The higher he climbed, the more odds and ends his superior, the actual director, his fraternity brother Oberwieser, pushed off on him as his responsibility. Leopold was the steam shovel who scooped up the garbage. In the absence of Court Counselor Oberwieser he had to assume Oberwieser's agenda, as well as his own; but whenever Leopold returned from vacation, he would find all the documents for which he was accountable still lying there, untouched. Then Oberwieser would hand over the stack of files and say to Leopold: "You mind taking care of these?"

Oberwieser's mother had been a teacher and had always insisted on refined speech and unassuming appearance. Oberwieser's father, as a politician, had partly earned, partly manipulated his way into a significant bureaucratic job, and, as a bureaucrat, had retained the language he had loved as a politician defending the interests of the little people. Court Counselor Oberwieser, likewise politically active, if not at a very high level, used his father as his example and spoke the same lingo that his father had always spoken. In spite of that, his mother looked up to him as she had previously looked up to her husband in his rolled-up shirtsleeves.

To a great degree, Court Counselor Oberwieser's political activity consisted of lunch meetings with members of parliament, party functionaries, and other people from whom he wanted something or who wanted something from him. The size of his belly corresponded to the scope of these activities. As a bureaucrat he was just as enterprising as he was as a politician – he owed that much to himself. His enterprise and his inner softness resulted in the fact that, prodded from somewhere, he began to careen in all directions. He accommodated all the citizens' concerns and usually effected a favorable or at least tolerable outcome. But up to that point it was always a difficult path, since he had a hard time forming shapes from the fog that surrounded him. It was easier for him when the administrator in charge, an underling, was sitting before him in a discussion. During this time nothing was actually discussed, but the presence of the administrator had a catalyzing effect on the Court Counselor's thought processes. It sufficed that he could look at the administrator from time to time and say "Hmm?" He was more likely to discuss whether it was better to say "could" or "would." And when he had improved the final draft of the administrator's text, by changing "to help" into "to provide assistance" and "to complete" into "to bring to fruition," he serenely scrawled his signature at the bottom with a flourish. In the meantime, the administrator had to suffer other indignities: the effort with which Court Counselor Oberwieser dragged his corpulence hurriedly between the office, working lunches, and other events; the political battles which he steadfastly waged; and the ringing of many telephones had damaged his nerves and frequently caused him to put his right index finger in his ear, rotate his finger twice; and often, also without any special imperative, he would poke it in his nose. On all occasions he regularly wore a striped shirt, either black on white or black on pink, a red-and-blue striped tie and a gray striped suit. His hair was greasy and stood on end. Beneath his scalp, behind a furrowed brow, his thoughts went around in circles.

Day in, day out, the highest-ranking administrator was the last one scheduled for discussions. That was Counselor Navratil. Since Court Counselor Oberwieser was afraid of his own wife, he enjoyed discussions that lasted long after the end of official working hours. Anyone who wanted to get out of a discussion like that at a reasonable hour shouldn't come in with a succinct, workable ruling, because Oberwieser didn't understand those things – or else he thought it was presumptuous and would tinker with it endlessly. So you would constantly have to struggle toward some middle ground, between the shapes Oberwieser could see by himself and the fog that shrouded the boss's vision. Leopold's eyelid would begin to twitch. Whenever he threatened to collapse on this precipitous donkey trail, he would go across the street to the little food market and buy a sausage and a roll or a canapé as provisions for his journey. As soon as the marinated herring reminded him of the North Sea, he felt as if he were back on his feet. And when he ate the sausage and roll at his desk, whatever was lying on top of the desk seemed bearable. By late afternoon he was pacing back and forth outside the boss's door, waiting for the present visitor's departure so that no one could crowd in line ahead of him. While pacing, for the hundredth time he would glance over at several framed color reproductions of Austrian landscapes, with the silent longing to see the Danube water nymph rise up out of the Danube once more. But it would be a while before he saw her again. Once, as he took leave of Court Counselor Oberwieser after a prolonged and grueling meeting, his gaze fell on a decorative mirror in the boss's office, and he was startled by the two agitated jelly fish eyes he saw; his belly, relaxed as he stood there leaning forward, had grown from the snacks and sausages and rolls to the proportions of his boss's own tummy; his cheeks, too, had become fat, his slanted eyes looked as if they were squeezed by his fleshy cheeks, which, in turn, made his cheeks look even fatter. But sometimes, when he had finally locked his files away in the file cabinet, it took some effort for him to lift his hand to the doorknob, and before he opened the door he paused for a moment, because he had other ordeals ahead of him.

"So that's what this world is coming to, when women spend their time earning money instead of raising children!" his mother thought, as she passed by the hags on the corner of the Naschmarkt and the Getreidemarkt. He knew that was what she was thinking – she insinuated it often enough. And it was clear that Erika was the one she meant, because Erika earned money teaching while her mother-in-law was left to take care of the children. And what she couldn't communicate to Erika in words, she communicated to her through her cooking – she vanquished Erika through her cooking! All the while she barricaded herself in the kitchen behind her bowls and clouds of steam which allowed no one to enter.

Sunday dinner was her decisive blow. But she herself was the victim of an equal blow on Sundays when the boys took a hike rather than serve as canon fodder for her many dishes. At Christmas, according to an old custom, she prepared twelve kinds of baked goods. In those days you could only buy flour and oatmeal as ingredients, and so there were precisely twelve kinds of pastries, all made from flour and oatmeal. This incessant silent test of strength often wound up in bickering with Erika about something inane, and whichever one of them received the last wound in such a duel would wait that evening for Leopold to come home as her avenger. Sometimes both of them wanted to be avenged. He could anticipate all that upon his arrival home; but before he could say hello, he wouldn't know whether the reproach would first come from his wife or from his mother: "After all, you're the man of the house!" He was a man between two women who wanted to tear him to shreds at the slightest provocation:

"Eat some more, take something else," Grandmother urged Maria.

"No, thank you, I can't eat any more," Maria resisted. But no sooner had she said it than there was a ladle of mashed potatoes on her plate.

"You don't have to feed her, she knows how much she wants to eat," Erika interjected.

"Maria is shy," Grandmother insisted.

"She's not shy at all, but you'll make her shy if you continue to force-feed her."

"It's okay, I'll take some of it off her plate," Leopold placated them. But after dinner, when his mother had retired, he got an earful:

"You should have supported me instead of stuffing yourself with mashed potatoes."

"I don't see a conflict where I need to support someone. People don't need to make a mountain out of a molehill of mashed potatoes."

"We're not talking about mashed potatoes, we're talking about who is going to raise our children – your mother or I. And who is going to have the last word in this house – your mother or you."

"What do you mean? If I do what you want, I'm the man of the house. And if I don't do it, I'm not?"

Erika pursed her lips and left the room. She needed the first couple of steps to catch her breath, then, from the next room, she would begin to complain out loud. Leopold took a deep breath and went into the kitchen to get his beer and wash away the words he wanted to get off his chest. On his way to the kitchen, he ran into his mother, who was fuming:

"You don't have to think that I'm going to take it when Erika insists that I'm intimidating her children. You can tell her for me that her remarks were out of place."

"I don't think I need to discuss with her right this moment if our children are shy or not. Marie isn't shy, so you can't have intimidated her. And that's why I think we can just put this issue to rest."

"Nevertheless, you can tell your wife that just because I look after her children, I will not let myself be blamed for ruining their character. And you can also tell her that I heard it when she slammed the door earlier, and that I also know why." And she slammed the door of her room behind her.

It was pointless to try to appease her. Erika really had slammed the door harder than she should have. If you didn't believe it, then you were just a pantywaist who was afraid of his wife. And his mother had taken out after the younger woman, if not snapping with words, then with a look or with a sharp voice. And if you didn't believe it, then you were just a pantywaist who was afraid of his mother. Gradually the silent reproach in the eyes of his wife and his mother which he encountered upon his arrival home changed its substance: not that he was the man of the house – their glances signified that he was no man at all, or simply that it was a shame he was there at all. So he cowered under their glare, hugged little Helli who laughingly threw herself against his tummy, and kissed the cheek of the maturing Maria who avoided his kiss when he tried to hug her. Sometimes he was at least able to appease his children. When he heard one of them cry out in her room "Give me that!" then it was Helli who wanted something; if a voice yelled "Put that down!" or "That belongs to me!" then Maria was protecting her territory. At the dinner table a compliment on a particularly tasty soup could also thaw icy expressions for the time being. But only when his mother had carried out the dirty dishes, when he himself had accompanied her, ready to help, to open the doors and clean up any leftovers, and when he had poured himself a glass of beer in the kitchen...then his own time had come:

Raising the beer glass in a welcome salute, reciprocated by a host of faithful followers, he entered the room from which all traces of dinner had been removed and approached his throne beside the standing lamp. He sat down, took a swig from the glass, put it down beside him and reached for the book that was waiting for him, while the faithful stood reverently behind him. When he opened the book, the faithful disappeared into the fog from whence they had come, always ready to reappear when his thoughts should summon them and to support his opinion unanimously. "That's the way it is!" was his opinion when he read about the villainy that had occurred in the past two decades and made the world what it is today. There was Hitler, in his bunker, writhing in a fit of rage and in seconds enflaming thousands of his soldiers; there were Roosevelt, Stalin, and Churchill, dividing nations among themselves. "Roosevelt didn't give a damn what was happening to us, but we're voluntarily becoming Americans," he said, and the faithful behind him nodded their assent.

And tanks were still threatening the borders of Saint Leopold's domain. They came out from under the credenza, driving up and over the edge of the carpet. But when their treads tried to climb the border and the tanks raised up, exposing their vulnerable underbelly, they were mercilessly dispatched by the faithful, entrenched behind the flower tendrils. Then the tanks' wreckage was strewn on the parquet floor like dead June bugs, an obstruction to the columns following close behind them. But time and time again replacements were able to advance under cover of the wreckage, and suddenly they clanked forth, right through the arabesques in the direction of the ornament in the middle of the carpet. But they weren't going to make it. Forced to detour past the flower tendrils, they became entwined in the scrollwork at the ends of the tendrils, and like the seed pods of those weeds we call dandelions, they flew into the air when they came into contact with a leaf or a blossom. Similarly, the ones that advanced directly in the path of a blossom or a leaf also were blown away. "Welcome to my empire. Here you can feel safe and protected," he called to Erika when she came through the doorway, took a pile of books and notebooks from the credenza, and sat down at the table. But she put the school workbooks off to her right and commenced checking the homework.

The first workbook was Zelenka's, a girl who dragged herself from test to test with the greatest effort. Would she ever succeed in applying her knowledge in a practical way? Then there was Prihoda. She didn't drag herself, she was dragged – by her father and an army of tutors. She knew English well enough to run off to England or to America. Then there was Fräulein Holzinger, pale in her eyeglasses, who wrote her homework the way she might write a legal brief. They couldn't do any more for her intellectual development, since she was already smarter than most of the teachers, and that certain something she lacked she couldn't get in school. As Erika put the workbook down and leaned back in her chair to take a couple of deep breaths, she asked herself why she had been feeling so poorly lately. And lo and behold, out of a sea of blood and fire, a cannon barrel was aimed at her: from out of the book in Leopold's hands a feeling of disgust shot past her. She sighed and went back to work.

Later Leopold closed his book, put it down, and picked up his empty beer glass to take it out to the kitchen. In passing would he say something about the Americans we all are about to become? He hid his wisdom behind sealed lips. Soon thereafter she could hear him undressing in the bedroom. Then she too stood up, to take one last walk through the apartment and make sure that everything was in order. The children were asleep, the front door was locked. Just for the sake of thoroughness she turned the kitchen light on one last time. Everything was just as it had been earlier – the only difference was that now the beer glass was standing on the cleanly washed little table next to the sink, sticky with blots of foam and a yellowish coating at the bottom. It stood there every evening like that, she had seen it before, she was used to it. And she was sick and tired of it. She grabbed the glass and threw it on the floor. Then, after a half-embarrassed, half-relieved glance, she took the broom and dustpan and began to sweep up the sticky pieces of broken glass. Suddenly Maria appeared in the doorway in her nightgown, blinking sleepily: "What's the matter, Mommy?" "Nothing, go back to bed – good night!" The child stared briefly at the pieces of broken glass and then went back to bed. When Erika came into the bedroom, Leopold was almost asleep. She could have asked him not to defile her clean kitchen with his dirty beer glass. But then she also would have had to admit that she had just smashed his beer glass to bits. So she didn't say anything at all.

Every day, before she sat down to grade homework and prepare lessons, Erika went into the children's room, put her arms around her two girls and listened to their concerns: "Grandma said, if we yell, the *boogieman* will come," she found out. "Look over there, there's the nice *boogieman*," Erika said, and reached for the Negro doll that had been around since Leopold's childhood. "And when you yell, he'll come and say 'You sweet children, why are you yelling? Did someone hurt you? Or are you just fighting amongst yourselves? You don't need to fight with each other, because you've got so many pretty things!'" Whenever she was able to dispel one of her mother-in-law's monsters, it was a great triumph. If she stayed home all day and raised her children by herself, then they would never hear such foolishness in the first place.

Since the end of the war, a steadily increasing stream of new wisdom has engulfed her. The Americans paid for professional journals that regularly arrived in the mail in friendly envelopes, postage paid. She read a great deal about adolescent sexuality, about non-violent education, about democratic methods of instruction, about complexes and aggressions. No matter how often she had to shake her head at some of these ideas: after all she had had to read during the war in praise of everything that made children tougher or stronger, it was a revelation to her that now people could think or even write about things like that. And behind all these mental contortions, her "Oh, I see!" when confronted with the simplest facts, credibility with which all that she had read was repeated and her dreaming of solutions to problems which up till now she hadn't been aware that they even were problems – the image emerged of a slender, blond young man who had been in Vienna a long time ago to learn to solve problems, with his look of constant amazement, especially when Leopold had polished him off on the tennis court. Two postcards he had written her after his return to America were still lying in her desk drawer.

She was looking for a confidant to celebrate her victory over the *boogieman*, but Leopold ignored her mute invitation when he came home. Later, as Leopold was ensconced in his leather arm chair and had tried to capture her interest with an interesting quote just as she was sitting down to her work, she looked down at her homework notebooks. For the rest of the evening, each of them was preoccupied with their own thoughts. But the next morning in school, at some point between classes, two bright eyes behind their glasses frame caught her searching glance – they were the eyes of her colleague Trude Kulnik who taught French and German, a bachelorette over thirty with delicate skin and a mop of dark curly hair. It was so easy to say to her: "I really ought to spend more time with my children, this is a time when they really need me." Or "In the evening my husband is always so worn out." Or "My mother-in-law is so hard to get along with, I can't stand to live under the same roof with her." Or simply "That does it, I've had it up to here!" Trude's eyes reflected exactly what she had said, simultaneously full of understanding and a lack of understanding: Trude understood that such problems exist, but she had no way of understanding how good or bad the news was that Erika was sharing with her. Trude had no such problems – she read modern novels and watched French movies in the original. And when she listened to Erika, another pair of dark eyes peered out of her dark eyes, behind which muddled thoughts danced around until over the years they finally came to rest – sitting across from Erika in the person of Trude was a mature Rosi Lemnitzer who now listened to Erika just as Erika had listened to Rosi so long ago.

That changed. One day after school was out, Trude didn't walk in the direction of the streetcar, but across the street to the coffee house where a gentle Germanic-looking young man was smiling at her. Several weeks later she handed Erika a card stating that Helmut Wiedmayer with a degree in civil engineering and Dr. Trude Kulnik announced their engagement. And the next time Erika tried to tell her that "My husband is so worn out again," she noticed that it didn't have the usual effect. You couldn't just serve up some trite half-truth to a woman who now had her own husband. She would see through it, that the most important thing was concealed behind the tiredness and the complaint. So Erika didn't say anything, she just invited Trude to go to the coffeehouse the next time that they both had a free class period. Sitting there, staring into her coffee cup after rehashing some undigested thoughts, she said:

"Tell me something. I'm not a very good penitent, but I don't have a father confessor for my question. Do you think it's a sin if someone is proud to own a man?"

"Hmm, I don't know. Are you proud of owning a man?"

"No, not really. But do you think that it's a sin?"

"I don't know. It's probably not a sin, but maybe a shortcoming. At the very least it's cause for disappointment, because no one can completely own another human being."

"I'm glad you said that. I'm also glad that no one can do it. I never really wanted to own my husband. But when I think back to the time we were first together, it seems to me as if I used to be proud to own a man like that – even though I never have owned him."

"You shouldn't blame yourself for that. Do you think about things like that a lot?"

"No, somehow that just occurred to me while we were talking. When I'm alone, I don't think about much. More things occur to me while I'm talking."

"I don't think that something simply occurs to you if you're not aware of it. I just think that you're not being honest with yourself. How can you be proud of owning your husband if you've never owned him?"

"Well, you see, this is the way it was. We were sitting under a pine tree in the Sparbach zoo, making a wreath of flowers. I told him a story about flower elves. Then he put his arm around me and said something hilarious, that he would put my flower elves into a salad bowl. He was also a good tennis player – at least he used to beat good tennis players – and he was a good-humored young man, too. And all of a sudden he was standing there in front of me as if he were on a pedestal, as a beautiful specimen of a man, as lord and master. Not that he was actually beautiful, but when I saw him like that, for me he was the standard for masculine beauty. And at that moment I felt: and now he belongs to me! It was a dumb feeling, I know."

"That is a dumb feeling, no doubt about it. As far as you were concerned, he probably had the same feeling."

"When you put it like that, then I would have to say yes, he definitely thought that I belonged to him."

"And when you tell me the story like that, then I would say he was posing in front of you in order to win you over, and you let him win you over. I can't imagine where your feelings of guilt come from."

"I'm glad you said that."

"And now he's the happy owner and is still proud of it. I'm afraid you let him own you to the point that you've become convinced that your marriage is a property situation. And since you're not satisfied with that kind of relationship, you feel guilty because of your involvement, even if you are only a passive participant. That's a laborious task, because he, as the unsuspecting owner doesn't have a guilty conscience. – You can tell I used to translate legal texts."

Upset, Erika drummed her fingers on the tablecloth and then ordered two pieces of apple strudel.

"I hope I haven't been unfair to your husband with my know-it-all comments."

"Yes and no. In some ways you're right, but not entirely. If owning means to roost on something and keep it caged, then he doesn't own me. He prefers to roost in his easy chair and wrap himself up in his own daydreams. He generally reads books about the war – I can understand that. After all, he had to take part in it. But I get sick to my stomach when I see the airplanes and guns on the cover. And sometimes he seems to be thinking about something in his imagination. I can tell from the look in his eyes. To tell the truth, we live in two different worlds."

"And does he talk about it with you?"

"Rarely. Once in a while he condemns the Americans because they bombed Vienna – preferably when I'm reading something American!" In saying that, she had raised her voice. She realized the situation now that she put it into words. For the duration of this thought she stared past Trude, off into space. Then she asked: "Can guns also shoot backwards?"

"I don't know, but I can imagine that they build them today so that can't happen. Why do you ask?"

"It was just an idea," Erika said.

They continued eating amicably. Then Erika ventured another question. "Where did the two of you meet?" And Trude began her story:

"At ski lessons last winter. He was so nice and could ski really well. During the first warm days in June, one afternoon during the week, we went swimming along the Danube meadows. We hiked along a sluggish tributary of the Danube, between willow trees, in sun and silence. There were giant sycamores all around." She gazed upward and leaned back in her chair. "Suddenly we stopped. A naked goddess stepped out of the thicket right in front of us, crossed our path, and disappeared behind a stand of willows along the bank. Then we heard her dive into the water and swim away. We walked on. From her beach towel, bottle of suntan lotion, and a bag with clothing we could tell that she hadn't been some mythological Danube water sprite after all. We saw her swim off, her hair tied up on top of her head. A little further on, where the thicket opened up to a sheltered area, we put down our bags. I took off my sandals, my eyeglasses, and shook my hair out. He smiled at me. Then I took off my belt and unbuttoned my dress, and took off everything I was wearing. And that was that."

"Your dress is lovely."

"You really think so? It's quite old – actually the oldest one I have. But I really like your dirndl."

Erika became bold. "Do you know what we'll do? We'll trade! I'll loan you mine and you loan me yours. For the longest time I've been wanting a red dress like that with green polka dots! Just for a few days – or even for a few hours!"

Trude enthusiastically agreed, and they returned to school. After the last class, they hurried over to Trude's nearby apartment, straight into the bedroom with the unmade beds, and traded dresses. "Look, it fits me! And your sandals would fit, too!" Erika was ecstatic as she pulled up the zipper. "Take them with you," Trude said. Then they kissed each other on the cheek, and Erika ran home. The whole day she felt an elation that she tried to put into words but couldn't. That evening, when she was about to go to bed, Leopold was already lying there, his back toward her. She announced: "I went to confession today."

"What did you confess?"

"That for years I have been guilty of wearing high heel shoes that were too small for my feet."

"Aha!"

Leopold was wide-awake. Why was she hurling this confession at him? What did her high heels have to do with him anyway? He was silent, and his silence crushed even him. But his silence enveloped this tidbit she had thrown his way – the two collided with a dull thud. Tidbit lay beside tidbit.

He heard her toss her clothes on the chair. She must be standing behind him, naked, in the nakedness of her pride that hides nothing.

He awoke sometime during the night. What had she really confessed and to whom? Why was she bragging about it and yet concealing from him what it was really all about? What would happen to him if he went to confession? But off the top of his head he couldn't think of anything to confess. Besides, he couldn't fit in a confessional. But more than anything else, a man who was sitting on his throne shooting up tanks didn't have time for confession.

In his dreams vague antagonisms and unspeakable qualms weighed heavily upon him. When he got out of bed the next morning, he truly didn't know what he had dreamed. He could only remember that everything had taken place and yet not taken place. Erika had appeared to him in the dream – he wouldn't have recognized her if he hadn't known it was her. In his dream she had looked completely different than in real life. Burdened with uncertainty, he went to his office. But it was a relief to return to his normal self when, at the lunch break, a young man approached him on the street, smiled at him, put his hand over his heart in a greeting of peace, and bowed deeply before him. It was his fraternal brother, Dr. Alfons Altenweil. As he approached Leopold, the pavement beneath his feet was transformed into a carpet that his great-grandfather, as ambassador, could have afforded at an exclusive shop. His smile was embellished by a mustache, the kind worn by someone who at his morning ablutions would gaze into an Empire mirror whose frame would tolerate neither walruses nor seals. "Hello, peace be with you," Altenweil greeted him in a clear and mellow voice, as if he were still surrounded by the velvet curtains that muffled the tone of his voice in his parlor. It was a portable parlor, it encompassed him wherever he happened to be. "And may peace be with you, too," Leopold answered, as he had learned in the pages of Karl May. "To what do I owe the pleasure of our meeting? I see you've been shopping."

"Yes," Altenweil answered, inhaling. "I'm temporarily a bachelor and do the shopping during my lunch break."

"Then this evening you must come and share a modest meal with me which my spouse will prepare."

"Delighted," Altenweil assured him, bowing yet again.

Erika had just taken off her apron and dried her hands when Altenweil rang the doorbell. He was carrying a bouquet of flowers that made Erika's eyes pop. Then he bowed before her to kiss her hand.

"May I kiss your hand, madam. My dear friend, your husband, was so kind as to invite me on such short notice. I dearly hope that I will not tax your hospitality." That said, he presented her with the bouquet.

At that point Leopold spoke: "May I introduce my fraternal brother, Dr. Alfons Altenweil – his wife is out of town for the time being."

Erika thanked him for his greeting and for the flowers, assured him that she was delighted that he could come, and asked to be excused since she still had a great deal to do. The two gentlemen went into the living room. Erika placed a teapot, a plate of sandwiches, and the flowers in a vase on the table and hoped the gentleman enjoyed the meal, as she once more lovingly arranged the flowers – a colorful resplendence of carnations, buttercups, chrysanthemums and other cultured wild flowers. Then she went into the bedroom and sat down with her books and homework, and was pleased that she was such a sweet and gracious wife.

After they had eaten, Leopold selected a leather-bound volume with gold lettering from the bookcase and said to his guest: "Look at this. I've got a beautiful book that has a picture of your grandfather."

It was a lovely edition in art nouveau style with gold embossing about the celebrated exploits of the Austro-Hungarian army in the First World War – a charity edition with proceeds to disabled veterans of the war. Leopold opened it and pointed to a photograph that depicted a general with his soldiers in the trenches. "There we are. You can see him right here, our very own General von Altenweil."

Dr. Altenweil produced a face that implied "Oh, how interesting!" and said: "Yes, I'm familiar with the picture and this book. My grandfather apparently acquired it himself. As a boy I often looked at it, until one day I closed the cover and said to myself: That's the end of that!"

Leopold took the book that was the end of that and placed it back on the shelf. Something melted within Altenweil, and he continued:

"Thank God, my father never tried to force me into following in the footsteps of my glorious forefathers. He could clearly see what was past, and he placed great emphasis on living a simple life as a landowner on his estate. He proved his military skills by bagging his annual limit of deer and rabbits, and I resolved my father-son conflict with him by never doing it myself. From the tours of the estate with our forest warden I knew every individual animal species, and I never could bring myself to shoot at any of them."

"We don't kill our own veal schnitzel either."

"Exactly. I just went off into the woods and built my own outlaw hut and played cops and robbers with the boys in the village. My father was all in favor of that, the way you're in favor of a child playing with dogs and cats so that he learns how to get along with them. For the same reason he also approved when two of my classmates, Franzl and Karli from Kremsmünster, and I joined 'Vogelweide,' instead of joining my noble cousins in their authorized regional fraternity. You'll see, he said, you men of the 'Vogelweide' will either go to the dogs or be for the birds – at least as far as my father in his noble tolerance was concerned."

"It doesn't matter. It was your good fortune and ours."

"Certainly it's been my good fortune. I know people whose greatest concern is to remain true to themselves. And they do that by constantly setting themselves apart from their contemporaries on all sides and by fitfully identifying themselves with their ancestors back over the centuries – which means that they identify themselves with a few scraps of parchment that they can't read, with a rusty suit of armor that doesn't fit, and with a few family myths that aren't true."

Staring straight ahead, Leopold pondered for a moment. Then he spoke more to himself than to his conversational partner: "It's just good when we know where we belong – after all, we are the product of our ancestors. A long time ago I was involved with a Jewish coed, but something came between us. In any event nothing came of our relationship."

"Yes, certainly. If you don't belong somewhere, you usually notice it yourself, or others let you know. If neither of the two happens, then you can assume that you belong right where you are."

Leopold could feel the burden on his chest, the certainty of knowing better and the uncertainty of what it was he knew. Altenweil reinforced his own conviction with a swig from his glass.

Around ten o'clock Erika was still in the bedroom and could hear the two men go into the hall and Altenweil tell Leopold to inform his dear and most gracious wife how grateful he was for her wonderful hospitality. Then the door opened and she could hear their voices echoing on the stairway.

"You're supposed to tell me how grateful our guest is," Erika said when Leopold joined her in the bedroom and paced back and forth several times.

"Yes, of course, he wanted me to thank you and tell you how much you impressed him. You've acquired a new admirer."

"That's good," Erika thought.

The next morning the children asked their mother where the beautiful flowers on the table came from.

"Our guest brought them for me yesterday. Do you like them?"

"Yes, because they're so pretty."

"An elf lives in every flower. During the night all the elves come out of their flowers and dance in the moonlight. Each elf resembles her flower – the one in this buttercup wears a splendid dark-blue dress, and when she dances, she slowly hovers; if you try to catch her, she immediately disappears – her name is Maria. And a funny little elf lives in this marigold, she wears a yellow little dress and skips over the meadow, and if you try to catch her, she dances around on your nose. Her name is Helli. We have to give the flowers fresh water everyday, or else they'll die of thirst."

"Then the elves fall out of the flowers and into the salad bowl," Leopold said. And the children laughed.

The door to his mother's room, usually always closed, was now wide open. Glancing into the room caused him to inhale with pursed lips and exhale with mourning, memories, but also with dwindling trepidation. The bed was empty, her coffin was closed.

"She ran out of time, and I am running out of space," he thought, as he stepped out of the bathroom and looked down at the expanse of his unclad body. Erika shot past him in the direction of the bathroom door. "Now we've got more room in the apartment so that I can expand better horizontally!" he said to her, but she was already gone. Helli came out of her room, cast a sharp glance at her naked father and disappeared into another room. (He had already seen her, naked as a jaybird but with makeup, bounding from the bathroom to her room. She was taking ballet lessons and enjoyed looking at herself.) But as for Leopold himself: not just in the bathtub, his consecrated pool, which, according to his own blueprint was built in the former storage room, but now in the expanse of his apartment, he too could enjoy himself just the way God, in His enormous goodness, had created him.

They all had more room to breathe. The now-empty room was painted for Maria so that she could create her own world in it. Till now the two girls had gotten along halfway decently in the room they shared – at least they had argued at a similar decibel level. Each could now evolve more fully in her own room. Helli usually left her door open, Maria shut hers. Helli left her things lying all over the whole apartment, then would run from one room to the next looking for something important, all the while nibbling on something from the icebox. Maria put everything in its place and stayed within her own space. When their father came home, Helli would let him give her a peck on the cheek, Maria stayed out of reach. Helli practiced ballet movements between the bed and dresser, though Maria didn't practice anything of the sort because she couldn't do anything of the sort; she had taken piano lessons as a child, of course, but she hadn't touched the piano since the day when her fingers were too stiff and uninspired to play the Haydn sonatas. Maria rarely let a boy lure her out of her shell, whereas Helli often went out with one of her many admirers. And one evening her father watched as she allowed a companion to kiss her at the gate, only to escape and disappear inside the front door.

At the same time Maria moved into her new room, Erika had the old odors of plain home cooking scraped from the kitchen walls. Then the walls were painted a sunny yellow, and the kitchen cupboard was replaced by a cabinet with a work surface. After that she attempted to try something even more daring: she bought vermilion paint and covered the old kitchen table, the matching chair and the kitchen wall shelf with it. She put the table and chair in the corner off to the right by the window and hung the shelf above them. The books and workbooks she needed on a daily basis she placed on the shelf, her writing utensils went in the drawer. And at the bottom of the shelf she fastened a swatch of coarse linen as a wall covering on which she used pins to stick up whatever was important to her: notes with important deadlines, schedules, and postcards. At the very top she hung two old postcards which had been lying in her briefcase for a long time. They showed scenes of Philadelphia and a small town in Pennsylvania. Written on the back was "Cordially yours, David."

"You've set up a lovely Little Brooklyn here!" Leopold said, admiring her new realm, and she could tell that he knew exactly that the postcard was not of Brooklyn, but of Philadelphia. Three days later Father Leopold, sitting down to dinner with wife and daughters, said:

"Roosevelt and the Russians divided Europe during the war. Roosevelt let the Russians have the part they occupy today. The difference between the two is that the Russians believe they're doing us some good, while Roosevelt knew that he was doing something bad for Europe. And if a bomb had killed us all during the war, it would have been an American bomb."

"Why are you telling us that now?" Erika asked.

"Just so that you know," Leopold answered.

Court Counselor Oberwieser retired. Senior counselor Leopold Navratil succeeded him as office director and was appointed acting Court Counselor. Now he could relax. The twitch in his eyelid disappeared, his belly remained.

Now he could lean back at his desk and stretch his legs. But he ran into some resistance – Philipp Mattauer began to throw a monkey wrench in Leopold's well-oiled machinery. The Ministry, under Mattauer's signature, rescinded Court Counselor Navratil's decisions without clarification and without any relevance to everyday life. Mattauer didn't have to know anything about life, because he was the stronger of the two and had the minister on his side. Subsequently there were also directives signed by Department Head Mattauer. And after one such draconian directive, when Court Counselor Navratil had ground his teeth and issued a draconian reply, it came to pass that Department Head Mattauer ruled in the final instance that the party in dispute was found to be in the right, with a justification that would have occurred to Court Counselor Navratil too – if only it had occurred to him.

Court Counselor Navratil had once again conquered his after-lunch drowsiness and begun to study the incoming petitions, grievances, and directives, when a woman, a Dr. Bakos, phoned and requested that she be allowed to speak with him in person. A moment later she entered his office. She was pretty and smiled like someone who wanted something that she couldn't get just by asking. He was pleased to have seen through her ploy and pleased that he was one of those people whom it paid to smile at. So he smiled back at her. The woman, Dr. Bakos, wanted something for her illegitimate child. This child had a more difficult time than other children, because its father, a medical student from the Congo, had disappeared in the turmoil of that country's civil war. Court Counselor Navratil listened with an uneasy feeling. According to the law and in the opinion of the Administrative Court, he had to say "no." But to have to say that to a woman, face to face, induced pressure in his chest and abdomen. He was left with the thought that he had done his duty, a duty that slowly revived him internally, coupled with the regret that he had had to do his duty...and with loneliness in tragic proportions. The woman, Dr. Bakos, grimaced and left, either to look for a new benefactor or to take her case to the ministry.

When the secretary announced that a Dr. Ildiko Bakos was there to speak with him, Department Head Mattauer expected to see a pudgy person with disheveled dark hair. But when she entered his office, he changed his mind: she was dark after all, but slender, and he found her face interesting. She presented her case (which dealt with her illegitimate child) and told about the father (the Congolese student who had disappeared). Department Head Mattauer didn't quite understand, so he said: "First of all, I want to congratulate you for raising or having raised your child under such difficult circumstances. Unfortunately, too many mothers – or so-called mothers – resolve this problem by taking the easy way out."

"Well, abortion is definitely not a possibility for me. That is due to a kind of religious conviction of mine that a child has a right to life, even if it hasn't been born yet. After all, a woman can feel it in her own stomach that it's there, and how it stirs, and that it wants to live."

"Yes, I'm sure no one understands that better than you. I wish everyone understood it that way. I hope that you and your child haven't had to suffer from your fellow man's lack of understanding."

"Yes, from time to time. But we can live with it."

Mattauer leaned back in his chair. Around the chandelier ran a stucco laurel wreath. It was silent. "Perhaps you are about to have good luck in your bad luck – in other words, in your difficult circumstances. At least now you know who your real friends are. But, please, we must return to the problem at hand. My good friend and colleague with whom you've spoken, Court Counselor Navratil, is an excellent legal scholar and, in any event, has thought a great deal about his exposition. And the judges on the Administrative Court are predisposed against your request."

"Do you know that I myself am a lawyer and want to ask you if there isn't a precedence whereby I am right according to its basic premises." She quoted a ruling from an entirely different field of law that Department Head Mattauer wasn't familiar with.

"I don't know if we can squeeze much out of this ruling. But there is one other precedence that might possibly help us out a bit..." and he cited a ruling of the Administrative Court that Dr. Bakos wasn't familiar with. She detected that he had made a concession and simultaneously shown that he was the cleverer of the two. So that was a good beginning.

"People can always see things from two or more perspectives," she said. "The same thing happens to me when I take photographs. Actually I was a professional photographer before I began my studies, and I still take pictures for pleasure. By the way, I really like this photograph."

It was in a silver frame on top of a bookcase. Department Head Mattauer liked it, too. A colleague had taken the picture at an official social function, and the entire department had presented it to him on his birthday. It depicted him, leaning back in an armchair, his mouth half-open, pointing at something with three fingers. "I can see that you are opening your mouth, preparing to express a thought, while formulating an explanation with your hand."

"I am delighted that you see it that way. I suppose I see it a little differently. I'm afraid I wasn't thinking anything at that moment and wasn't formulating an explanation. The crush of people was too great for any of that."

She rose, went over to the picture, and examined it a while longer: "You don't have to think or to formulate the whole time – you are pure thought. You must have experienced a lot."

She was certainly right about that. He had armed himself to fight for his homeland and found out that it was all in vain. He had been beaten up, had endured hardships and fears despite hunger and exhaustion, had consoled himself during the whole ordeal with his love for his far-away wife and with her love for him. With an empty stomach and aching limbs he had called to God from the depths – and God had answered his prayers. And now he no longer understood God. The Biblical Job had risen from the manure pile, had looked around and seen the others croaking on their own manure piles. He exhaled the grace that had filled him and let it waft away like a misty breath on a cold damp morning. What kind of God was that, who so blindly tossed His grace amongst men? "According to God's will we're all together again, let us be thankful!" his mother had prayed at their first family meal following his return. If God had wanted him to be free, then He had also wanted him to be imprisoned, moreover had wanted that millions of human beings were to die or become criminals. And he, Mattauer, should be thankful for that? Still, he couldn't get around it. He had borne his agonies in God's name and thereby survived a few breaths longer than those who pitied themselves and quarreled with God – about those crucial last breaths.

God wants me to accept my beatings, he had thought. His enemies had said that God wanted them to beat others – because God wants the extermination of lives that are not worth living. As a result some of them were hanged for their own extermination. Their God had forsaken them and had gone over to the other side. "Incidentally, the Trinity is a postulate of the theory of cognition," Leopold Navratil had once revealed to him, with his elbows and pudgy cheeks filling the entire breadth of the table on which a bottle of Krems wine stood; the bottle had reminded Leopold of a picture of the Trinity by a master painter with the name of Schmidt and prompted him to utter several unassailable pronouncements about creation, revelation, and conscience. "Be careful that God doesn't escape just when you think you've got Him safely stored away in your botanical specimen container," Mattauer had answered him. Sometimes, on a clear evening, on his way home past St. Stephan's cathedral, Mattauer would fly from the base of the tower up to the pinnacle, toward God, through solar systems and Milky Ways, through thousands and millions of years, to the depths of the universe where He no longer wore any of the masks that people here on earth had hung on Him. But whenever Mattauer tried to grasp Him, his hands caught something else: star dust, primeval mist, or some indefinable twinkling. And when he abandoned this daydream, discouraged, he was suddenly standing at the base of the tower again, solidly on God's creation and at the place that God had allocated for him and him alone. All about him people were running around, with their wounds, boils, and welts, just as he had suffered them himself. If he could free one of them from their suffering, he would fulfill God's will, and God would have helped that person. A nurse, for whose children's home he had once intervened with a troublesome office, wrote: "Things looked pretty bad, but the good Lord took care of everything just fine." Finally, I have discovered the truth – I myself am the good Lord! Why didn't you tell me this earlier? He turned away from the tower, a blackened head looked out over him, and he then went in pursuit of destiny which would take him where he and only he could prove himself, where he could give something that no one else but he could give, or where he could attempt something that no one other than he could attempt. And if, for a time, he didn't stumble onto the extraordinary, he did as much as possible at his desk so that he wouldn't suffocate under the weight of the ordinary. He would demolish verbal constructs that had lost their basic meaning, or put a question mark beside a compelling summation to motivate the author to think, just once, beyond his competence. If this way he could spur on the bureaucratic horse or force it to leap and bound for his own amusement, then in the evenings in the theater with Christine at his side he could let the passions of the heroes and the thoughts of the poets pass right by him, and he comforted himself with the thought that at least in the theater every crime had its punishment, every leading note its triad. And now he was leaning back in his armchair, with his mouth half-open, his forearm propped on the armrest with three fingers in the air, only to let them fall without a word, which meant: there are certain basic principles to which we must adhere! And simultaneously: basically there are so many things that don't change, things we would like to set in concrete with our laudable principles. Because you can best tackle the little things in life with a flick of the wrist. One blow more or less, one piece of bread more or less – you survive one way or the other.

"The photographer has captured a good likeness of you."

"In any case at least you are consistent and don't say: he captured your real likeness. Because when something has several sides, there is not one single correct perspective."

"No, except perhaps of a sphere or of a cube. But I only take pictures of living beings, primarily people, but sometimes dogs or cats, too; they are much better than people because they always appear as they are, not distorted by shirt collars or a crease in their trousers. For that reason, when I photograph people, I prefer to do portraits or photograph them in the nude."

"In that case, I'm afraid I would be a big disappointment to you."

"Don't say that. People are human beings, and you can photograph each of them that way. And a photograph is not a finished product. People change. What was true yesterday doesn't have to be so today. When I'm involved in something and don't know where to turn, I take a picture of myself with a self-timer. The picture will tell me if, at that moment, I am up to the task or not."

"As a portrait or in the nude, if I may ask?"

"Either way. You can tell from your facial expression as well as from your posture how you stand in relation to the world and its challenges. I've also done photo series of friends and acquaintances, and they helped them. We all need to see ourselves and each other the way we are."

"Yes, I'm sure you're right. But, in any event, your assumption must be validated by the results."

"If you're interested in results, I'll be glad to show you a few of my pictures. If you would like to drop by my place sometime – I live right nearby."

"Hmm, yes, I would like to. But I think we should first come back to the basis for our conversation, and I would say we should terminate it for now. I'll ask Assistant Department Head Janschitz to take another look at your request. He'll give you a definitive answer. And then... I would like to drop by, whenever it's convenient."

He had never met a woman like her, and he had never heard or said anything like that. What was behind their small talk? Apparently he still hadn't completely lost his curiosity about people. And what do you know! He began to ponder a human being again, for the first time in a long time.

He put Dr. Bakos's petition on Assistant Department Head Janschitz's desk: "Say, do you mind taking a look and see if you can't find a favorable resolution for this party. The matter is somewhat problematic, but it seems to be a welfare case concerning a child with a Congolese father who has disappeared." Assistant Department Head Janschitz slaved over it for an entire afternoon, and in the end he was successful. Appropriate notification was forwarded to Court Counselor Navratil.

When Court Counselor Navratil had perused the document concerning the Bakos case, he slammed his fist on the table and had his secretary make an appointment to speak with Department Head Mattauer immediately.

He entered the outer office. "The Department Head will be right with you, he is on the phone. Please take a seat," the secretary said and went to the door to indicate to the Department Head that he had a visitor. Navratil could hear Mattauer's voice from the inner office: "But that's terribly nice of you, Herr Minister, to set aside two tickets for me – and free passes, on top of that! That's a pleasant surprise!" A surprise that he seemed to be accustomed to. Court Counselor Navratil clutched his fists and tugged at the waistband of his trousers.

"Well, hello! It's really nice that you've found time to come for a visit," Department Head Mattauer greeted him with open arms. "Please, have a seat. Will you drink a cup of coffee with me?"

Court Counselor Navratil would drink a cup of coffee. The maid-of-honor came in. Just a moment ago, at her telephone and typewriter, she had been a part of the system; now she was a woman – her smile was not a part of her job on behalf of any old citizen, but was reserved exclusively for the guest. She presented the tray with coffeepot, two small portions of milk, a sugar bowl, and two coffee cups. The host raised his hand with palm upward, indicating with a smile the lady who was his lady but who now belonged to his guest for the time that it took her to place the tray on the table and lay out the place settings. Then she poured the coffee and milk and left the room, smiling. The host's hand had followed the serving girl's walk to the table, had gently accompanied her movements as she poured the coffee and then approached the sugar bowl; she had touched the bowl with two fingers and pushed it toward the guest: please, help yourself! And, following his host's gesturing hand, the guest turned first toward the noble handmaiden and then down to the table and the sugar bowl, and, as it glided across the table toward him, he bent down to the bowl and to the hand that had pushed it: "Thank you."

"You're welcome!" Mattauer also took a sugar cube, admitting that he too was a man who lived from food and drink. And when he reached for the spoon, Navratil found himself grinding his fingernails into his palms.

"How are things with you?"

"Fine, thanks. The state is still resting on its legal foundation, and we'll survive along with it. But not long ago you sent me a directive that has overturned my entire previous modus operandi. And if, in the future, we administer justice according to principles like this, we'll have the Administrative Court or the Comptroller's Office on our necks."

"I know you're referring to Frau Bakos. In her case I'm neither afraid of the Administrative court, because she would have to be crazy to complain to the Administrative Court about a ruling that was in her favor – nor of the Comptroller's Office, because they don't have enough personnel to check an insignificant case like that. Besides, the ruling isn't as frivolous as you seem to think. And, finally, the lady is a type of welfare case."

"Well, excuse me, but in my opinion this directive is the most blatant perversion of justice that you've ever requested of me. I, too, would like to have earned a little kiss from the lovely Frau Bakos. And if you here in the Ministry believe that's how we dispense justice, then just give us the appropriate directives and we'll proceed accordingly. But I never would have inferred a ruling like that based on all your previous directives – not to mention based on the law."

"I think we can continue with our established procedures: you decide what you think is right, and we'll tell you if it was correct."

"I am appalled! We shouldn't treat Frau Ildiko Bakos any differently than Frau Ilona Nagy or Frau Etelka Perezlenyi!"

After a vehement dispute, an image of reconciliation: it was pleasantly transformed by the Pannonian vineyards, caressed by the glances of dark-haired female petitioners. And just look at that – Department Head Mattauer was actually smiling. But appearances are deceiving: he was smiling at Court Counselor Navratil's rule of law:

"You know, the consummate rule of law can be a monstrosity."

"I've lived through a time when there was no rule of law. I've seen bombs fall and half the city be destroyed – fortunately they spared your home."

"I've also lived through that time and acquired some rather vivid impressions. We have no choice but to make the best of our experiences. Obviously you share the general antipathy to the principle of 'Regulations are regulations.' It doesn't hurt if we have a few rulings that don't fit into the general picture, as inspiration for exceptions."

"But how does this inspiration work? Your thoughts about the Bakos exception don't have anything in the world to do with the next exception. In the end we're left with a mindless administration."

Mattauer chuckled into the distance. "You mean the state would then be governed by a blockhead dressed in a pin-stripe suit – by a Minotaur?"

"Exactly, by a Minotaur. And it wouldn't take long before it gobbled up the citizens and the state, too."

Mattauer gazed past Navratil: "Look, I could use my official position to pull rank and give you a directive. Or I could just talk nonsense with you – that would be comfortable and would sound like dry humor. Or I could just say nothing because what I want to say is somehow awkward for me. But I would like to explain what I really feel: that you and I are two deformed old geezers. We think that our servitude has made us victims or heroes or whatever. But in reality it has only deformed us. We can't be allowed to pass on our deformities to others and certainly shouldn't believe that they give us an entitlement to be correct now and forever. As a young man I wanted to fight for justice for my trampled Austria. Now that I've escaped from hell alive, I have to ask myself what, in fact, justice is, and who deserves it. Was it right that I was imprisoned while the biggest scoundrels were allowed to run around free? Or was it right that I survived while others perished? It's better when I don't even think about it anymore and just make sure I don't cause anyone else to brood over injustice in the world."

"And are present and future generations supposed to patch together their legal codes out of this chaos of rulings that you're cobbling together like this?"

"The present generation can use me as their excuse all they want, whenever they want, and I won't try to convince future generations of some particular ideal of justice that I don't have, since it was beaten out of me."

"And for that reason you're willing to forego law and justice altogether? Then who is supposed to understand them, if not you? The civil servants who use you as their excuse? Or your children whom you don't want to deform?"

"Not my sons, for the time being. The older one is telling everyone he meets about Isolde's *Liebestod* – he's probably in a late-embryonic stage – and the younger one hasn't shared his views with me yet. But someday each of them will decide what to make of life, or at least find a recipe in some cookbook. A clever Chinaman, who is home in my display case, once said: "When inspiration is absent, there is always compassion; when compassion is absent, there is always justice; when justice is absent, there is always the law. I've chosen compassion as my recipe for living and try to make that do, especially when it come to attractive young ladies."

"An unusual approach for a civil servant with a legal education."

Mattauer refilled his coffee cup and dropped a sugar cube in it. "You were always a great fighter for the law and for that reason want to replace the perfect unjust government that you despised with the perfect just government. But *summum ius, summa iniuria* – total justice leads to total injustice. In the case at hand you may actually be right. Perhaps my protégée doesn't even deserve our overly generous benevolence. Not simply because I want to fall back on my right to make rulings, but precisely because I'm not certain which of us is right, I want to get really personal with you, as inappropriate as that may be. I've already indicated some of my own defects, so now I won't have to bring them up again. But as far as you are concerned, you are so unrelenting on behalf of your good intentions as formerly Hitler was for his evil ones. You administer justice based on your thought constructs. You justify these constructs with your unerring and competent intellect as the final authority. Meanwhile you overlook the fact that your thoughts are driven by your emotions, just like all human beings. For that reason you are an intellectual. As long as an intellectual only torments imaginary subjects with his thought constructs, he is harmless. But when a construct like that is applied to real flesh-and-blood people, it becomes dangerous. And – pardon me for saying so! – the kind of people who come up with such airtight constructs are people who need a protective shield. Why do you need that kind of thought-shield? Hitler is dead, may he rest in hell; the Administrative Court won't do anything to harm us; and the Comptroller's Office would never dare to take something away from a black child."

"Thanks for the splendid lecture. Apparently I'm not afraid of you either, because otherwise I wouldn't have come over here to let you talk my ear off. And whether I'm afraid or not, I still will take the chance and show some intellectual backbone in my rulings."

"To be more precise: I don't mean that you are afraid, I mean you have angst. Angst makes intellectuals. And if you can free yourself from it, you can still use your intellect to play tarok."

"I play a mean game of chess."

"There, you see. So now we can agree that we can take the occasional appearance of a lovely petitioner as a reason not to make our administration into a steel corset that we force future generations to wear. We see things in our own way, and at any rate our children will certainly see them in their own way. And the various images of things we notice don't really say all that much about the things themselves, but more about us. If you perceive in that line over on the wallpaper the contour of a female breast, you're a sex fiend. If you see threatening, gaping jaws, you're a coward. As you may have noticed, I am alternately both. If you see in the woman who served us our coffee a goddess who pours nectar and ambrosia, you're an Olympian; if you see Frau Tomaschek, you're a mortal. And even if someone should say 'How can you see a goddess in a completely ordinary woman?' – that someone is obviously uninspired and needs to be kissed by the horse of the muses. Tell me what you see, and I'll tell you who you are. So let's not be so rigid, and we can hope that future generations will see the world in a different light than we do – maybe one day in the way its Creator really intended. As an old friend, that's my advice to you."

His words snuggled up to Navratil and stuck to him. Leopold wrestled free. Mattauer noticed his misgivings:

"For my part, I promise you I will restrain myself from continuing the trend of my rulings that you've contested. Just keep fighting for our constitutional state – then you'll surpass me in the end!"

Court Counselor Navratil was partially satisfied because he had made his point after all, partially reconciled by Mattauer's partial concession. Peeling away the last remnants of the words sticking to him, he bowed in leaving, as a Court Counselor is required to do in the presence of a Department Head. Then Navratil walked down the stairs, at first with pursed lips in resignation, then with clenched fists of resentment, and at the bottom, on the last step, gritting his teeth with rage: just the way he had bowed before Mattauer once before as he was being led to the police station by a two-man escort – and that, after Leopold had just accorded Engelhofer a similar gesture of subservience. Could he never escape his submission?

And there were other things he could not escape. No longer constantly bound to people and things, more and more often he slipped to the point where everything threatened, surrounded, and trapped him. Previously he had gotten vertigo just by looking up at the tower of St. Stephan's – now he got dizzy just by looking up the spiral staircase of a four-story building or even from looking down from the fifth floor. "What's wrong with you?" Erika asked him on the way to the Wiedmayers' apartment when he couldn't climb the first step in their staircase, but was able to begin climbing only by looking upwards, feeling his way from step to step, up to the third floor. "Nothing, I was just looking," he answered and turned around, happy to be torn away from the adventure. At the Wiedmayers' the words "children...stage play...schoolwork... savings" went right in one ear and out the other. But when Helmut told about a bridge construction project he had designed for export to Bulgaria, Leopold interjected: "You know, some day Russian tanks are going to cross that bridge. With a pair of binoculars you can see the Russians from the Laaerberg. I could see through the telescopic sight on my anti-aircraft gun how the Russians were advancing from Hungary while the Americans were still dropping bombs on us. Did you have to report for duty?"

"Yes, near the end I was drafted as support for an anti-aircraft gun. And when things really got hot, a couple of SS-guys put a machine gun in our hands and told us we were to stop the Russians in their tracks. Then they took off. When they were out of sight, we took off, too."

"Then you certainly must have noticed what all happened. But you were probably too young to notice."

"Yes, I was too young for the whole thing," Helmut answered.

A while later Erika asked him if he couldn't take off the day after tomorrow – at school the principal was holding conferences, and she had made a date with Trude to take a day trip to the Vienna Woods and to take their husbands along because it was prettier and quieter there in the middle of the week. "I told her you definitely didn't have time, but, since Helmut is coming along, she insisted." Leopold made time. So the four of them climbed uphill over rocks and sunny spots, beneath pine trees. Suddenly an explosion boomed from the nearby limestone quarry. It pierced Leopold to the core. "Aren't you feeling well?" Erika asked him. "Thanks, I'll be all right. But when you've heard that in the war, sometimes it all comes back to you." At noon they sat down in a beer garden on the hill. Sitting across from Leopold, Helmut gobbled up his lunch as if he had a bib around his neck. Leopold cut loose: "You childless couples don't know what it means to build bridges in Bulgaria so that the Russians can cross them in their tanks. Some day they will be in Austria. In the end our children will find out what it's like. Just take a look from the Laaerberg over to the east, then you'll see how quickly they can be here!"

But Helmut replied, as jolly as before: "Dear Leopold, first of all the Russians aren't faster or slower getting from Pressburg to the Laaerberg when I build a bridge in Bulgaria. And, second, an invasion would affect our children just as it would yours – because Trude has been expecting for two months now!" Hearty congratulations and toasting followed. When the two couples parted, Erika vigorously reprimanded Leopold: "You know how you started in on Helmut today – that was more than just tactless. And he is such a nice man. And Trude can't help it that she hasn't had any children till now." Leopold stared at the ground and didn't say a word. As they climbed the stone steps to their apartment, he let Erika and her wrath go three steps ahead, and, looking down at his feet, searched for drawings in the stone: the jaws, goggle-eyes, and monsters that had held him spellbound and haunted him as a child. He found them again. That night he dreamed a muddle of shapes and figures, abysses, and people who confronted him in a hostile manner and couldn't be approached – even Mattauer was among them. And at one point he heard thunder. He woke up and asked himself if the black bird – half-rooster, half-raven – was sitting on the edge of the bed, and if the seven dwarves would come to his rescue.

"Hey, what are you looking for down there?" It was his fraternity brother, Assistant Head Newerkla. Just then Leopold became aware that he was standing over a sewer grating, trying to peer down through the holes into the shaft. "Did you drop a five-schilling piece down there? Forget it – let me buy you a cup of coffee, and then you'll be even again." In the café Assistant Head Newerkla asked: "What are your daughters up to? They must be about old enough to get married."

"Thanks for asking. Thank God, there's no talk about getting married yet. Sometimes admirers show up at our place – the most recent one was a Palestinian, but we haven't seen him for a while now – and that doesn't bother me. He didn't leave any bombs behind, at least none have exploded yet."

"What did Erika say about him?"

"She'd be glad to let any old gypsy in, because on the Statue of Liberty in New York it says that 'all men are born equal.' The Statue of Liberty is her American college friend with his psychology textbook in his hand."

"Say, are you jealous of your wife's college friends? Whew, that would sure keep me busy. You know what? Just to cheer you up, we could all go together this year to our fraternity dress ball, and our Toni could open it with your Maria."

"Fine, agreed." And Leopold was back in his good Court Counselor-mood. "I can see that you folks in the Ministry are just as clever as you look. In general it's easy for you to be clever, because the parties just complain to you when they think the lower departments have done something wrong. When a party is satisfied, the Ministry doesn't hear a word about it. For that reason the Ministry isn't familiar with the real practice of administration, but nevertheless thinks they are cleverer than the lower departments. Actually, someone ought to collect the rulings of the Administrative Court, as well as those of the lower departments." "That'd be a fat file," Assistant Head Newerkla objected. "Doesn't matter, that's why we have computers nowadays. When the European computer production gets in high gear someday so that we don't have to pay exorbitant prices to the Americans for every computer, then we'll be able to afford them." The next day he called in his deputy, Dr. Wondrak, and assigned him, together with the younger interns, the task of perusing all the files according to their basic rulings and compiling an index of these rulings. Several months later, at one of the fraternity's discussion evenings, he gave a brief presentation on the necessity of collecting the basic rulings of the lower departments, when he said, looking directly at Department Head Mattauer: "In reality there are no prescribed channels of appeal in the administration at all, from a subjective standpoint. Every civil servant who makes a ruling has his own conscience as the ultimate authority, in which case he must allow for, dispose of, or avoid certain obstructions if they get in the way of his ruling. For example, if a civil servant must decide where a road should be built, and he wants to build where there is a cliff or where a directive prohibits it, then either the cliff will just have to go or the directive must go – that means he must make every effort to achieve a repeal of the directive. In a worst-case scenario he can also squeeze his way around the cliff or the directive. Whether he is successful or not is, from his point of view, merely a question of doing it. Seen from the perspective of the political conscience, there are no lower departments. There is no hierarchical structure within the legal system!" The pyramids of norms and channels, turned upside down, collapsed in a heap. But Department Head Mattauer spoke with a smile: "From today onward, we in the Ministry will have to keep a close eye on you chaps in the lower departments!" That was the extent of his contribution to the debate.

Following the discussion, Leopold strolled home, exhilarated. He greeted Erika, sitting in her study corner, as the most beautiful of women, poured himself another glass of beer, and drank it in little swallows as he paced back and forth. "Mattauer got upset today when I started pecking away at him!" he laughed in the general direction of Erika as he placed his empty glass on the sink. "Don't you want to wash it out and put it back in the cupboard?" she asked. This rebuke ruined his victory celebration. "Of course, you're right. You women have to bring your husbands up properly. Sometimes monkeys are easier to tame, and Americans even easier. Trude will soon have Helmut trained. And I'll do everything in my power to follow in his footsteps."

"Don't keep picking on Trude and Helmut. He's not some trained monkey, he's a man who looks after his wife. And if you don't follow in his footsteps in this regard, some day I'll run away from you."

"Then I'll just sit here calmly and wait for you, because when people panic they always run straight ahead, and since the earth is round, one day you'll come back to me."

She looked straight ahead, indifferently. Then she said with an indifferent voice: "Your good humor will crack beneath you like a sheet of ice in the warm winds of the spring foehn."

"What do you mean by that?" he wondered.

"Think about me, when the time comes," she answered.

Maria was sitting in the middle of the room in her white ball gown, in makeup, with her hair parted down the middle (though she never wore it that way at any other time), waiting for her escort. At eight o'clock Toni Newerkla arrived, a miniature Voltaire in the grace of his salutation, the smartness of his glance, and in the length of his nose. The sash and beer-drinking cap of his fraternity made him appear more coquettish than down-to-earth. He helped Maria into her coat, accompanied her down to their taxi, and rode with her to the Sofia ballroom where the cotillion of young ladies and young gentlemen were gathering.

It was a family party. When the parents arrived a half-hour later, young and old friends were pressing around the cloakrooms, and wherever they looked, they were greeted warmly. Court Counselor Navratil put his hand on his wife's shoulder and pushed her ahead of him through the smiling and laughing melee; at the stairs he took her arm and led her up to the loge that they had reserved together with the Newerklas. The latter were already there and greeted them from a distance. Assistant Head Newerkla had bequeathed his sharp facial features to his son – of course, the father looked more earthy, more like a lumberjack – and Frau Newerkla had donated her smartness which made her look maternal and vivacious. She got along well with Erika, since the two of them were English teachers.

Accompanied by the blare of the Fan Polonaise, the cotillion of young ladies and young gentlemen entered, with Maria in their midst, her gaze scanning the floor, carefully striding step by step while the nose of her squire pointed the way. On the heels of the polonaise came the opening waltz, followed by the public waltz. Leopold asked Erika for the first dance. In high spirits, he was looking forward to an especially exhilarating treat. But time and time again they bumped into other couples and each other; sometimes they stumbled. After the dance, in the throng of people, he stroked her back once, down to the point where the curvature fit nicely in his hand. Scarcely anyone noticed that her shoulders and the corner of her mouth winced. Then Leopold plowed through the dance floor with Frau Newerkla, while Assistant Head Newerkla danced with Erika. After this exertion they all met back in their loge and opened a bottle of wine that had been standing on the table since they arrived. "When the weather's nice again, you really must come to the Scheiblingstein and drink a bottle of our red currant wine with us," Frau Newerkla said. The inaugural couple appeared, everyone congratulated them with "You danced beautifully!" and offered them a glass of wine. As they all leaned back, contented, Dr. Alfons Altenweil entered their loge. He asked Court Counselor Navratil for permission to dance with his charming wife, and led her to the dance floor. To her obvious delight, neither her talent nor enthusiasm on the dance floor irritated him. Then Dr. Altenweil also danced with her charming daughter.

In the meantime, from his loge Court Counselor Navratil observed the dancing couples – especially the female dancers. He felt that their various temperaments were exposed through their various styles of dancing: the snake wrapped herself around her partner and fluttered her tongue in his face; a lanky lass resembling a beanpole let her partner push her around the dance floor and bumped into his knees; Frau Newerkla, in reverse gear, created turmoil among the other couples, just as she intended, despite her partner's failure to lead her as he intended; with a dumpy stride and figure, a chubby Viennese woman stumped past. And then Maria appeared out of the crowd, once again with Toni Newerkla. Court Counselor Navratil would have been almost irritated, because she seemed to dance so lethargically – after all, hadn't he paid for her admission ticket?! – if she hadn't looked so cautiously intense, like someone completely immersed in the dance. She tried to follow her partner without colliding with him, and danced each whirl only as far as she had to, so that she didn't get in the way of his sweeping strides. She went along with his movements, not to complement them, but to avoid them. The redness on her cheeks, from the heat or excitement, said: "This far, and no farther." Court Counselor Navratil saw a salamander who, with lethargic but well-measured steps, moves through the foliage and with the gleaming of its markings fends off whatever could come too close to it. One more thing attracted his attention: from the other side of the dance floor two frogeyes stared intensely into the ballroom. They were the eyes of another young fellow who belonged to the fraternity, his name was Mühlhofer or something like that. Through his horn-rim glasses with God knows how many diopters, he gave everyone in his line of sight the feeling that they were being stared at. His broad face and low forehead with the slick black combed-back hair contributed to the effect that people perceived only his fixed gaze. In this manner he stared out into the ballroom – somebody had probably liberated his date.

Toni returned Maria to the loge. She retrieved her handkerchief from her purse and wiped the perspiration from her forehead and neck. Her father poured her a glass of soda water. Then he asked her to dance, and she danced around him just as carefully as with her previous dance partners. Afterward they had scarcely sat down when Erwin Mattauer fitfully pushed his way into the loge entrance, greeted everyone tempestuously, and asked Maria to dance. He was Department Head Mattauer's older son, chubbier than his father and more intense in his speech and gestures. During the waltz to the left, he just whipped her around in circles. Department Head Mattauer danced too and blessed the masses with a smile so thick that anyone could slice off a hunk and take as much as he or she wanted. Maria disappeared for a while, then reappeared with Otto Hornik, one of the sons of the dead fraternity brother Ulrich Hornik. The poor man must have stepped on that fatal mine with the same kind of stride that his son affected while dancing. Peter Mattauer, Department Head Mattauer's younger son, slender and polished like his father, also danced with Maria.

After midnight Leopold danced with Erika once more. On the way back to their loge he slipped his hand down over her hip and noticed that her cheeks had a redness similar to when they had glowed beneath the pine tree in the Sparbach zoo; this same red glow could also be seen on Maria's cheeks. Erika's face betrayed no emotion. On the other side of the ballroom Mühlhofer was still or again staring out, trying to locate his vanished date. Court Counselor Navratil thought: "Yup, old buddy, that's life" and nodded in his direction. Around one o'clock the two sets of parents went home and relinquished the loge to their young ones.

Frau Newerkla's red currant wine beckoned magisterially, and the Navratil family obeyed. "You've got to come along, or else Toni will be disappointed," Frau Newerkla said to Maria. Maria wasn't terribly excited about first being skewered by his nose and his compliments and then having him talk her ear off – but that wasn't a suitable excuse. So she too hiked up to the Scheiblingstein.

The sun was shining between the brightly shimmering beech trees onto a forest floor that was free of underbrush and only covered by a thick layer of leaves. If you walked beside the path, the leaves rustled. Slowly the Navratil family climbed up the forest trail. At the top of the hill they came to a clearing in the woods, a restaurant appeared and gardens spread before them. It didn't take long to find the Newerklas who greeted their guests warmly. The table in the garden was already set with tea cups and dessert plates. Toni spoke surprisingly little and primarily flattered the already buxom Helli who enjoyed it immensely and laughed unselfconsciously at his attentiveness. Maria stretched out on a recliner and hid behind a glass of red currant wine. On the other side of her self-imposed barricade the two fathers were talking about trade policies and the balance of payments. Their conversation pleasantly lulled her to sleep. But then Toni shoved his nose into the discussion and things began to get unpleasant – they got louder, uncouth, and sometimes two of them talked at the same time. After a while Maria was able to ignore the nearby fireworks and listen to the rustling in the treetops. As the sun began to sink, the Navratils said their good-byes and started homeward. On the way down, Maria found it more enjoyable to walk off the beaten path and to kick the heavy wet leaves into the air. Suddenly she saw at her feet a salamander lying in a hollow – it was black with glowing yellow marks. It didn't try to run away, its right front paw appeared to be injured, perhaps stepped on by the footfall of a tramping tourist. She picked up the little creature who hardly resisted, placed it on her left palm and covered it with her right hand. She had already decided to take it home and nurse it back to health.

Next day she bought a glass container, covered the bottom with sand, put a saucer from a flowerpot inside for drinking water, placed the salamander in this dwelling and set the whole thing in the living room under the little flower table where it was not too bright and some of the leaves hanging down from the table would simulate a bit of nature for the salamander. Every evening she would fill the saucer with fresh water and serve him a leaf of lettuce or other leftover vegetables, and garnish it all with the vinegar flies that had gotten caught in the net covering the fruit bowl in the kitchen. Then she watched the salamander as it gradually pulled itself along step by step, all the while a strange fire glowed from within it and could be seen through its markings.

Whenever Maria looked up from the pavement or from her desk in the lecture hall, more and more frequently she began to notice numerous pairs of men's eyes looking at her. When she stood in a window alcove between lectures at the university, young men strolled over or crowded around her. She was being courted.

Toni Newerkla showed up at her home to take her to the movies. "A nice young man," her parents thought. He took her on his scooter to the movie theater, and there she saw dunes, a woman's body glistening from the sand, and a hut where a woman and a man tormented each other. Afterwards, in the bar, Toni contemplated the bubbles rising from his Campari and said: "We've just seen again how we men are nothing without women. To some degree we consist of what women put into us, and to another degree of what women drag out of us. Because for us, ourselves, we consist of what we see of ourselves reflected in women. If someone takes women away from us, then we lose the ground beneath our feet and fall into the abyss of our masculine reason. We remain there as a mute corpse. Basically our life's utterances are all aimed at women: when we cry, we're crying for our mother. If a male can't hope that his mother will come, he can't cry. If he loves life, he loves it because he has learned to love a woman, and if he loves a woman, he loves her because he has learned to love his mother. For that reason, every man tries to find a woman who resembles his mother, and then his mother is jealous because she sees herself defeated by her daughter-in-law with the very same weapons, and doesn't understand that her son is only admiring his mother through his wife. Just as a husband hugs his wife, a baby monkey reaches for the fur on his mother's breast; and just as a wife hugs her husband, a monkey mother embraces her young. And women know how desperately we poor men are dependent on them, and they exploit it."

Maria didn't believe that. She was simply disgusted by the fur on the mother monkey's breast, and she felt the point of a drill aimed at her. So she said: "I don't think that's true." Then Toni took her home.

A week later Erwin Mattauer was standing at the door with outstretched arms, lowering them to pass through the doorway – it was, well, almost too narrow for him. He stretched his arms out again, preparing himself for a hug, but he only got a handshake. He took Maria on his scooter to the theater, to a studio play. In the first act the man and woman didn't like each other, in the second act she liked him but he didn't like her, in the third act he liked her but she didn't like him. By the final curtain they were both in love with each other.

"To be honest, it's blasphemous to write a comedy about love. It's on the same plane as when we laugh at Max and Moritz, shot full of holes, as they come out of the meat grinder in pieces. Love and death are so closely related, that's why we like to laugh about them. Love is death. Death is love – the *Liebestod* is the very, very oldest human desire."

Erwin took a sip of his vermouth to give her the opportunity to respond, but she was silent. So he put his glass of vermouth down on the marble top of the café table, looked into her eyes, and continued:

"In the *Liebestod* we are taken up into the eternal community of all people of all times. Everything that separated us from them disappears. The *Liebestod* is our predestination from time immemorial. When the hunter goes out with his hunting companions and is killed by a bear, his final certainty is that all about him his friends will fight for him and are prepared to die for him and with him. He is totally unaware that his death helps to provide his friends with venison – for him that is a matter of course. Then he's carried home, in a procession following the bear he's killed – the best piece of the bear will be buried with him in his grave. The bear's skull will have a place of honor at the banquet, afterwards it will be buried beside the dead hunter. That's how the hunter and the hunted are reconciled and can confront each other on the eternal hunting grounds. And the man who has survived every hunt dies in the cave beside his wife and children, loved right up to the final beat of his heart. In his last moment on earth, when he senses how he is assimilated by the loved ones around him – that was perhaps the most beautiful moment of his life. What we fear isn't death, but the fall into oblivion. Oblivion is the rejection by the beloved, the mother's first spanking, and the cry for help that goes unanswered. We approach death and love, we fall into oblivion. The rider from Lake Constance rode out to find love and death. He wasn't frightened of death, but of the fall into icy oblivion."

He looked into Maria's eyes, she felt a steamroller approaching. Consequently she avoided his gaze and said she didn't think it was true that love and death had anything to do with each other. Then he picked up the check and took her home.

Another suitor turned up. He had sat down next to her in a Spanish class and introduced himself. His name was Dr. Horst Sekeli, a marketing scholar seeking employment and learning Spanish on the side.

He rang the doorbell. Maria went to open the door, her father right behind her. Outside stood a short, sturdy man between twenty-five and thirty, a square head on a square body. His short-cropped hair, his glasses, and his eyes were black. He greeted them with "Hi," pecked in the general direction of the father (which was supposed to represent a bow), and spoke up at him in a lovely theatrical voice: "Good evening, my name is Sekeli. I've come to take your daughter to the movies."

"Enjoy yourselves," her father said and returned to the living room. Maria slipped into her coat, walked out the door with her date and locked it behind her.

"Do you know what you're going to do now?" she asked him, as they were standing on the front steps.

"No – I mean yes," he answered and walked more slowly down the steps.

"What does that mean?"

"Look, I can't explain it to you while we're walking, I'd have to stop," he answered. He stopped on a step, leaned against the railing and looked up at her. "In this world there are people who have something and people who need something. And there are people who have exactly what the others need. So I want to make sure that the people who need something get what they need, and, of course, from the people who have it and don't need it."

"I don't understand that exactly. It sounds so... Does that mean that you want to become a revolutionary?"

"Well, not exactly... a businessman"

They continued down the steps in silence. She could tell that he was continually staring at her from the side, but she was watching where she was walking so that she didn't miss a step in her high-heeled shoes.

"Look," he resumed, "it probably sounds manipulative, but it's the only way to help people get what they really need. It's really an art: first, to find out what people really need, second, to convince them they really want it, and third, to get them to the point that they'll also pay for it."

She began to understand. "And how are you going to find all that out?" Then she took his arm and supported herself on it so that she wouldn't start to wobble on the cobblestones. He walked her silently to the streetcar stop, then paused and spoke up in the general direction of the electric lines overhead: "Somewhere in Timbuktu there's a tin shack with a jukebox. The blacks continually throw money in it and listen to Elvis Presley. I heard that from somebody who was there. And when I asked him if there was any point to it, he said: 'As long as they've got the jukebox, they don't cause any trouble.'"

He looked back up at the electric lines. She waited to see if he was going to add anything to what he had just said, but he didn't say any more. So she asked with a slight reproach and yet shyly: "So you want to sell jukeboxes to the Negroes?"

At first he didn't respond. Finally he said: "No. But I want to find out if there isn't really something they need more and also what somebody could sell them."

The streetcar came. They got on and sat down across from each other. The streetcar started to move. They didn't speak until they came to the next station. Then Maria asked again: "But how are you going to find all that out?"

He took a deep breath. "There are brilliant people who are tearing their hair out over this. A few of them are working at the Institute for Social Sciences. They've got a position for an assistant there right now. And after I've been there awhile, I'll be just as brilliant as they are."

"And what if you don't get the position?"

"Then I'll go to Düsseldorf. Not long ago at a Heurigen a pretty young woman from Düsseldorf told me that the people in Düsseldorf are Germany's elite. Can you imagine how happy my father would have been thirty years ago if he had known that someday his son might belong to Germany's elite. I'll definitely find a position there. I'm just happy that I'm in world trade and not in law – that way I won't get any crazy ideas because of my career choice. Not long ago I read about a case where an innocent man spent five years in jail. If I were that man, when I got out, I'd kill the judge, his wife and children in the most brutal way possible!"

He had raised his voice in a threatening tone. Startled, she stared at him face to face, then she looked down. He didn't say anything else. Shortly thereafter they got off the streetcar and went to the movies. They saw lions hunting, sunsets over the steppes, lovers' dilemmas, and heroism.

It was a mild summer evening when they came out of the movie theater. "Come on, would you like to take a little walk?" he asked. She nodded and took his arm again. First they strolled across the Ringstrasse and through the Volksgarten, and then strolled into the inner city. Neither of them spoke. She gazed at the sidewalk, he looked half at the street, half somewhere up above.

"Hey, look at that!" he suddenly said.

They were standing in front of an antique shop. In the illuminated display window stood a peasant chest with roses on a turquoise-blue background, a Baroque writing desk with inlaid wood, and a Baroque table with some painted glasses. On the walls hung pictures of Biedermeier scenes. In the back, a plaster Baroque cherub blew into his trumpet.

"How do you like that?" he asked.

She silently observed the beautiful objects. Again he stared at her from the side and noticed that the tenseness which had been evident on her face since his arrival and had remained there as the marvelous lions, rhinoceros, sunsets and couples in love flickered past on the movie screen, slowly dissolved. Perhaps it was the children playing in one of the pictures, perhaps it was the cherub who had accomplished all that. He began to relax.

"Of all those things, what would you like to have? The picture over there? Or the trumpeting angel? May I offer the most kind and gracious lady a trumpeting angel?"

He clasped one hand to his chest and drew his other arm to the side as if he were rendering a Spanish obeisance. Accustomed as he was as a short person constantly having to look up to other people, he stretched himself comically. And for the culmination of this farce he made a low bow, just like a rooster that scratches on the manure pile. A strange bandy rooster was standing before her. He and the trumpeting cherubim made quite a pair – one as comical as the other: the stocky little boy who was calling out Judgment Day and the little bandy rooster who wanted to sell the world its happiness. From within her liberated heart of hearts she was overwhelmed by a smile that was barely visible on her lips. In this instant he was overcome by the love of his life. She ended up loving her little bandy rooster even longer than that.

When the door had closed, the Court Counselor went back into the living room. He was overwhelmed by the realization: "This is getting serious." A guy like that had more permanent things in mind than some student in his third semester – and sooner or later Maria would get serious. But about this guy? He sat back down at the table.

"What does he look like?" Erika asked.

"Hard to say – dark, rather short, rectangular."

After dinner he got up, went to the bay window and peered out into the darkness. He could see the guy right in front of him: in any case he was different from Maria's previous suitors; they hadn't been right for her. Maybe that was why she approved of this guy. And he was a Ph.D., too. When greeting Leopold, who was twice his age, he had pecked like a black gamecock; he would have to see if there wasn't a predator hiding behind this bandy rooster. The black eyes beneath his glasses could be hawk's eyes. And all of a sudden this Dr. Sekeli craned his neck before the Court Counselor, made a bow, flung his arm to one side and spoke: "Best regards, Herr Subordinate Counselor!"

The Court Counselor's clenched fist shot up into the air. The other guy had disappeared. Did he intend to show his face again, the coward? There he was again, cutting his capers and calling out again: "Best regards, Herr Subordinate Counselor!"

The Court Counselor turned around, went over to his easy chair and lowered himself into it, with his fist still clenched. And once again the guy's mocking smile flashed before his eyes and crowed even more grotesquely than before: "Best regards, Herr Subordinate Counselor!"

The Court Counselor had no counsel. He couldn't escape this scarecrow here in his own home. If he stayed in his easy chair, the guy would come back, over and over again. And what right did he have to keep coming back? How dare he insult Leopold like this? Hadn't he, Leopold Navratil, refused to bow before the folks in the Ministry, and, after all, wasn't that the reason he had kept his position in the lower ministry? Had he ever chased after a swastika flag? As a student hadn't he traded insult for insult with the members of the dueling fraternities? Hadn't his classmates in school always been afraid of his ridicule? What kind of insult had he been exposed to here, and how could he sidestep it? If he kept sitting here comfortably in his easy chair, the slobbering fool could return at any minute. And then it occurred to him: he would have to chase him away. He would chase him to the furthest reaches of hell, where he belonged.

"I'm going to take a little walk. I haven't had much exercise today – bye!" he called out to Erika, slipped into his trench coat, and hurried out the door.

He rushed up to the Gürtel. A cigarette butt on the sidewalk pointed the way. It was dark tobacco, from a Pall Mall or some such brand – Dr. Square Head had tossed it away. With his foot Leopold kicked the butt aside and kept going, past an espresso. Through the window he could see inside: tubular steel furniture, the cheapest kind you can buy, an espresso machine on the bar, and a great deal of cigarette smoke hanging in the air above it – precisely the kind of place where this Dr. Sekeli would sit and smoke his stinking Pall Malls when he got together with his profiteering cronies to conjure up their shady deals.

Leopold crossed a narrow cobblestone street with low-slung buildings, through whose portals hay wagons used to drive three hundred years ago. Sekeli wouldn't feel at home around here. He hurried past several buildings from the late-nineteenth century, admiring their tall windows and grilled glass doors with company nameplates and informational signs mounted beside them. One advertised a law practice. Maybe Dr. Sekeli was a lawyer to whom you could go if you'd finagled an especially bad business deal? There was a printing shop and a trading company for import and export. Maybe that was something Sekeli would be interested in: he could take business trips and every time he came home he could smuggle in a carton of his stinking cigarettes.

The Court Counselor was feeling much better. In the narrow street with the Biedermeier houses where he resided, you could live well if nobody bothered you. But here, surrounded by late-nineteenth-century buildings with their portals and brass signs, you could do a great job of sniffing out Dr. Sekeli. Over and over again he examined the cigarette butts on the sidewalk; most of them were what remained of a pack of *Austria 3*s. But Sekeli could also have thrown away one or two of the other butts.

Then he turned to the left onto the Gürtel and headed for the

Westbahnhof. Paced by the green stoplights, bunches of cars shot past him like a horde of wild boars. It must be a Chinese torture for the people who lived around here, unless they had nerves of steel like this Sekeli guy. If he could chisel people out of the last of their possessions and drive his competitors to bankruptcy, if he could fly the coop while the police could only get their hands on his front man – a guy like that could easily tolerate this noise assault. Maybe he was just now sitting in that bar up ahead, negotiating with some supplier who had come from the east on the Orient Express, just waiting for the next outburst of noise before whispering his business terms across the table. Court Counselor Navratil entered the bar, sat down at a vacant table and ordered a beer from the taciturn, pudgy bartender. Then he looked around the place. The room had smoky brown paneling, the walls were decorated with a few advertisements for beer and other beverages. Over the coat hook hung a leather vest and a blue raincoat. Some men were sitting at wooden tables with beaverboard tops, silently drinking away. Their clothes were shabby like the whole bar. The bartender brought his beer. Court Counselor Navratil paid, emptied his glass in three gulps, and left. Outside, the streetcar arches were lower, the line disappeared underground, the Westbahnhof came into sight. Court Counselor Navratil crossed the busy Mariahilferstrasse, brightly lit by illuminated advertising signs, and kept walking along the Gürtel – once again it became a dark and destitute area, dominated by the spiked monster, the Maria vom Siege church that menacingly eclipsed the suburban buildings. The subway surfaced again and turned off over a steel bridge into the Wiental. Recalling the pathos of the working-class poets, working-class apartment houses lined the Gürtel in toward the city, while out toward the suburbs simple functional buildings predominated. There was nothing here that would be of interest to Sekeli, unless his grandmother lived in one of these community buildings, a woman from whom he would borrow money with the unshakable intention of not repaying it. There were very few people out on the street, the only evidence of life was provided by a couple of passing cars. In the distance the neon lights of the Südtirolerplatz appeared. Court Counselor Navratil hurried in that direction with long strides. When he got there, he turned to the right under the train bridge into the Favoritenstrasse. Here there were still people out and about. Display windows packed with practical items glowed from shabby buildings.

Juvenile tramps were hanging out at a hotdog stand. Court Counselor Navratil turned off into a narrow street on his left and walked past a row of new community apartment buildings. Several years ago there were still bomb ruins here, he could see them in his mind's eye: two boys were foraging in the bomb debris – a stocky, tough kid with a square head of black hair and a skinny blond boy. The blond boy had something in his hand. "It's mine, I saw it first!" the dark-haired kid screamed. "It's mine!" the blond boy cried. Then the dark-haired kid hit him in the face, and the two of them rolled in the debris, locked in combat. In seconds the square head was on top of the other boy and had snatched the coveted object away. Now the plain community apartment buildings came back into focus. A few hundred yards farther on, a shabby three-story house from the previous century was still standing between the newer developments. It had survived the war with its rotting window frames, its crumbling plaster, and its damp patches of mildew. A light was shining from a window on the second floor, a young woman in her slip appeared and then disappeared. Somewhere Sekeli was standing at her doorway, squarely in front of her. In desperation the woman resisted: "I can't hide you here, get out of my apartment!" "When I'm here, it's my apartment!" Sekeli persisted. Court Counselor Navratil quickly walked away, past dull new facades. Gradually he began to get tired, slowed his pace, and asked himself if it wasn't time for a break. All of a sudden, in a side street over a lowly old country house, he saw a green sign advertising an inn. Decades ago this street must have been a sleepy country lane, shaded by trees where the horses rested while the coachmen sat in the beer garden. Now everything was gray. The Court Counselor stopped. A jukebox blared from inside the doorway "Hang down your head, Tom Dooley, hang down your head and cry…" Navratil knew that it had something to do with a man who was to be hanged. A person who liked that kind of song would want to listen to it, and somebody who trampled a defenseless person would also be able to dance to it. Sekeli was sitting on the edge of the sidewalk in front of the inn. He was wearing a leather jacket and throwing a knife at the cracks between the cobblestones. The knife stuck fast every time. Beside him another guy was squatting limply, like somebody who long ago had given up on himself and the world. Sekeli was just telling him the joke about the father who promises his blind child that it will regain its sight if it will fervently pray to God. After the child has done as asked, but nevertheless remarks that it still can't see, the father makes fun of his child: "Gotcha – April Fools!"

"If ya don't laugh, I'm gonna hafta tickle ya," Sekeli threatened, and pointed the knife several times at the other guy's chest and stomach.

"Go ta hell!" the other man responded and punched Sekeli in the arm.

Then Sekeli plunged the knife between the other guy's ribs until he collapsed without a sound, and Sekeli took off running uphill to the Laaerberg.

Court Counselor Navratil ran after him.

He had lost sight of Sekeli, but kept running uphill to catch him. He rushed out of the crowded urban area, huffed and puffed in long strides along an unlit path up between the garden plots of the Schrebergärten, past the dark skeletons of the merry-go-rounds and other fair rides at the Bohemian Prater, up into the pitch-black oak grove at the knoll of the hill, struggled through branches, stumbled over stones and tree roots until, at the edge of the woods, he suddenly broke out into a clearing. The hill directly in front of him plunged into the unknown. He gasped for breath and stared out into the darkness of the plain that he knew was down below him but which was hidden from his sight by the night and an incoming fog. Gradually he caught his breath and his heartbeat returned to normal. He stood there and kept staring. But why? He had scarcely asked himself this question when it hit him like a bolt from the blue. Sekeli was there, bowing like some clown and crowing: "Best regards, Herr Subordinate Counselor!"

Court Counselor Navratil clenched his teeth and took a punch out into the void. Then he turned around, found the nearest streetcar stop, and rode home.

The next day he passed the time at his desk in the office. That evening he crept home.

"What does Dr. Sekeli do – what kind of profession is he in?" he asked Maria at the evening meal.

"He's applying for an assistant's position at a social-economic institute, or whatever it's called. If he doesn't get it, he's going to Düsseldorf."

"Social-economic institute – that could be a Commie job. He'll have to make friends with Engelhofer, if he hasn't already done so."

After dinner he went to his fraternity's meeting place where one of the fraternity brothers who had an important position in a nationalized business spoke about the economic prospects of nationalized industries. After the lecture they discussed for a while, and after the discussion's official conclusion a small group of very diverse people stayed on, gathered around the speaker: Altenweil, who was asking him about business connections of individual companies; Otto Hornik, who from time to time said something about economic theory; Court Counselor Navratil, who, on the other hand, was arguing that poorly performing state-subsidized firms were living at the expense of successful private businesses; Toni Newerkla, who contradicted him vehemently; Peter Mattauer, who was listening quietly, unmoved by the occasional agitation of the discussants; Erwin Mattauer, who understood very little of all that was said, but nevertheless announced that he was interested in economic problems because, in the final analysis, it was about the food and drink and air of the common man, ultimately even about the flowers on his windowsill; and Mühlhofer, who injected a few biting remarks about the in-fighting for positions in nationalized companies – apparently one of his relatives was in one such company. Court Counselor Navratil was even more delighted when he noticed that Mühlhofer's remarks embarrassed the speakers, especially when Mühlhofer accused Toni Newerkla of being an adherent of Austro-Marxism and when he compared Hornik's scholarly speculations with the writer Morgenstern's poem entitled "Palmström and von Korf calculate the cubic content of the Alps." By the time it was eleven-thirty, Navratil hollered: "Do you know what? Next week you can all come over to my place so we can continue our rowdiness!" The guest presenter excused himself since he lived in Linz. The others were glad to accept the invitation.

Court Counselor Navratil and Mühlhofer left the group at the same time. "You can really get those clever fellows all stirred up," the Court Counselor said in the hallway. And Mühlhofer looked at him with a sly glance.

Erika had retired for the evening, Maria was out with Dr. Sekeli, Helli was somewhere. Arranged on the table were seven plates, seven glasses, a platter of cold cuts, and a small basket of rolls and slices of bread with four two-liter bottles of wine on the credenza. The only thing missing was a good seating arrangement to stimulate conversation: if guests were comfortable at their seat, they were more likely to share their wisdom with the others. Toni Newerkla could be liberal if he was talking with a Socialist, but also when it went with his striped shirt, or he could be socialistic if he was flirting with a female sociologist. In the presence of a militant nihilist, on the other hand, he could cloak himself in clouds of incense from Gothic cathedrals. If Erwin Mattauer was within range, maybe he could fire off some surprising perceptions in his direction, and then his voice would resound from unfathomable depths like a wounded wooly mammoth. Otto Hornik and Peter Mattauer were able to situate themselves at the outer limits of Toni's field of fire. You had to keep Altenweil and Mühlhofer as far away from each other as possible in order to prevent awkward incidents. But maybe it was best to just let each of them find his own place and stake out his own territory.

They arrived one by one, each displaying his bodily coat-of-arms: Mühlhofer came in his frog face and spectacles – he immediately asked for a beer, and got it; Toni Newerkla was represented by his aerodynamic nose; Erwin Mattauer, his broad frontage, made even broader by his outstretched arms; behind him, one could make out his brother's smile; Altenweil brought his mustache and a bouquet of flowers "for your lovely spouse, with my greetings, in absentia." And last of all, Hornik with his lofty brow.

"Like the Seven Dwarves – the only one missing is Snow White. That's why no one has drunk from our cups or eaten from our plates yet. Nothing's been touched. Get your own drinks and help yourselves!" Leopold encouraged his guests: "Cheers!" And after a sip of the tart Poysdorf wine: "Now's the time we ought to sing the old fraternity songs, since we've got two prospective Worthy Grand Philistines among us!" Toni Newerkla and Peter Mattauer smiled gratefully. Leopold turned to Toni Newerkla: "Why, you've just published an article. What's it about?"

"It's about national economy and economic integration."

Mühlhofer butted in: "Say, that sounds a bit like a leftist aberration. Just be careful that you don't turn into a Communist, or else I'd have to bust your chops." Right off that was an awkward start, though somewhat alleviated by the fact that for some time now Mülhofer and his rude remarks had enjoyed jester's license in the fraternity. That he was tolerated by all his fraternity brothers he owed to those few good-natured Styrians and Upper Austrians who enjoyed his harangues and thereby provided the bonding agent to the other fraternity brothers. Of course none of the guests here was particularly interested in his caustic remarks, especially since they knew that he called them the "Schönbrunn Gang," probably because they spoke High German which he somehow perceived to be officiously Schönbrunn-yellow. His blast at Newerkla was intended to spatter the palace façade. But he detected the silent displeasure on behalf of the palace strollers; with a glance at his beer glass he emptied it and withdrew from the conversation. "Don't you want to try the wine?" Leopold asked him and poured him a glass. Mühlhofer raised his glass, said "Cheers," and drank. With that, Mühlhofer was accepted back into the circle of wine drinkers from whom he had isolated himself at the outset behind his beer glass. The others responded to his "Cheers" and thus greeted his atonement toast with their own acceptance toast. The peace that ensued appeared to do Mühlhofer some good, as well. He poured himself another glass, pulled back, and from that point forward limited himself to being a good listener.

Leopold turned to Peter Mattauer: "And what are you going to do when you grow up?"

"He's going to be the pride of the family. He's finished his doctorate, while his older brother is a perpetual student!" Erwin interjected, reaching over and patting his younger brother on the shoulder, which forced Hornik to duck his head.

"No, not yet. But I've applied for an assistant position at the Socio-Economic Institute. Whether I'll get it or not, only God and possibly also Engelhofer knows for sure."

Engelhofer, the mudslinger who had had Hitler looking over his shoulder! "Ah, Engelhofer, I know him well. When we were kids, he lived down there in the house next-door and we used to throw stones over the fence at each other. After that we went to school together for twelve years, and then to the university. Perhaps I could speak with him."

"Yes, please do," Peter Mattauer nodded, without aspiration or enthusiasm, rather slightly amused, both by the coveted position and by the proffered assistance. At this point he was the spitting image of his father as a student. His amusement was annoying, but you could disregard it by inferring that there was a good reason for it.

"A few days ago I saw an announcement for a lecture that Engelhofer is going to give, on the status of the progressive scientist or something like that. You've simply got to pledge to always be nice and progressive and socially relevant and to have status!" Everyone laughed, Leopold too – not only at his own joke, but that he was now going to sponsor Department Head Mattauer through his son as Leopold's protégé; he could smooth young Mattauer's way from the patriotic family tradition to a pink progressive future. In China the son glorifies the father – Leopold Mozart is famous as the father of Wolfgang Amadeus. The great social liberal, Philipp Mattauer, will become famous as the father of the great leftist-liberal social-science scholar and theoretician Peter Mattauer, immersed in a pink light by his son. The pink lamp illuminates from the bottom, and in its light the eyebrows cast their shadow upwards on the forehead so that the eyes look down somewhat more aghast at the strange little doctors who won't let their papers be torn from their hands, papers on which they have written their opinions with body and soul. He will be dead, this patriotic Christian and nobleman Philipp Mattauer, and in his place will stand the freethinker Philipp Mattauer who attained farsightedness and tolerance through contact with his socialist and communist fellow prisoners back in the concentration camp – an intellectual inheritance of Josefinism under new circumstances, a representative of that enlightened Austria that thinks in aphorisms, that abolished censorship under Joseph II and reinstated it under Metternich, that promises all freedoms and proscribes the funeral rites in order to show the small-minded pencil-heads what great things a great mind can allow itself to do. The former intellectual aristocrat Philipp Mattauer is dead – long live the new intellectual aristocrat Philipp Mattauer!

And yet something wasn't right. Had he actually ever been a Christian-patriotic nobleman – or anything else? He had never revealed it, at least not to his fraternity brothers and fellow students. He had always been in agreement with everyone else's opinion and had never revealed what he really thought. You could never tell if he was thinking anything at all. He may have been thinking about the voice of the soprano Jeritza, about his father's porcelain Chinamen, even about the rifle that the Ostmärkische Sturmscharen had put in his hand. In the office he had let the litigants and colleagues file past as if they were actors on a stage and he was the audience with a free pass. At home he had spooned his beef broth, praised his children for their grades at school, and given his wife pretty birthday presents. He had smiled all the while. He had been imprisoned in a concentration camp and gotten out alive, unchanged. He hadn't shown pain, nor had he been redeemed or enlightened. In church at court he paid his courtesy visits to his God. "Be careful that your God doesn't escape just when you think you've got Him stored away in your botanical specimen container!" Mattauer had once said. He had locked his God in the display case beside the family silverware, and He couldn't escape because silver-coated tin stayed put. The hedgehog that searched under leaves and thickets for mushrooms, berries, and insects had spread out his treasures before him and even put a bit of his heart into it, and the hare had courteously sniffed at it. He had never argued, never rebelled, never refuted outlandish ideas conclusively, because it was nobody's business what he thought. But at least once in his lifetime he would have to take a stand: when his son, ennobled to the rank of scholar with critical awareness and status, put forth his first fiery-red treatise. At least to his son he would have to say yes or no and thereby realize himself what he really was – if he was anything at all. You would never learn the answer, but through his son you can force him to come up with an answer, and you could bet on the outcome: it will be lodged behind his friendly smile – another smile – and then nothing, icy nothingness.

Words flew and arguments raged back and forth. Erwin Mattauer had an opinion on everything. Leopold turned to him: "And what's new with you? What's happening in the fine arts?"

"Well, I wish I knew myself! I'm still writing my dissertation on droll elements in Austrian folk literature...about the buffoon Hanswurst" (who poor Erwin would so like to be and would never be allowed to be) "...in his person he combines all the primal powers of mankind..." (being all things to all men) "...he preaches to us as a holy figure from Baroque altars..." Court Counselor Navratil responded: "Then we'll just have to canonize him, Saint Johannes

Wurst. In the canonization process I will perform the function of *advocatus diaboli*."

Leopold stretched out comfortably, enjoying the general merriment, and was pleased to have thrown a monkey wrench in Erwin's cothurnus. He drank another sip of peace of mind from his glass, leaned back and gazed up at the plumes of cigarette smoke above the table. Erwin's speech was up there and had dissolved in the smoke. Another cloud, emanating from Toni Newerkla, permeated and overlapped it.

"That is precisely the reason why your Hanswurst will always remain a utopia. With a morality that doesn't come from coexistence, but that lives in us only as a primitive power, life in any society would consist only of collisions of primitive powers! There is no such thing as a society of inspired Hanswursts, there are only Hanswursts in every society – buffoons who terrorize others with their primitive power or make others look like fools." And while the smoke clouds thoughtfully writhed and mingled with each other, Altenweil added:

"Above all, your Hanswurst is a poor fool, because he can't find forgiveness for his silly pranks. If you don't share a common morality with others, you can't apologize to them. When he sees that they are angry with him, either he continues to beat them over the head to punish them or he plays tricks on them out of atonement, leaps around in his own skin and exhausts his entire primitive power, continually in fear that he'll break through the ice on which he is dancing."

Through the ice – who was it who recently said that? Something was haunting Leopold.

Altenweil seemed to have convinced everyone – even Erwin couldn't come up with a rebuttal; to Leopold's delight, Erwin was obviously suffering. Puffing on his pipe, Newerkla exuded a further observation on the capriciousness of positive morality. Hornik thought that society had already tamed its saints who preached morality in its stained-glass windows, but folk culture remained multifaceted: "No sooner did we put St. Florian in his glass case, then the evil demon grabs us by our necktie from behind!" Erwin Mattauer slapped him on the shoulder, laughing demonstratively, and shouted: "You are the greatest!" Altenweil mentioned that St. Nicholas and his assistant Krampus shared a similar fate: we seemed to recognize ourselves in Krampus – that's why there are Krampus parties, but no

St. Nick parties. His words, caught up in the clouds of smoke, absorbed, engulfed, and dissolved each other. Toni Newerkla provided a flourish: "In any case, every race has its own folk culture which reflects its morality. And if we want to say something truly vile about a people, we call them a primitive race – as if there even was such a thing! And if no one believes this vilification, we allege that this race hadn't created their own culture, but simply borrowed one from some other race."

Newerkla's high, know-it-all tone of voice had a tedious effect, and the group began to have their doubts, probably also because an allegation can't be entirely correct if you need such a loud voice to express it. That was why they all listened when they heard Hornik's voice: it arose from beneath his eyeglasses, deep, slow, and resonant:

"That is why at least a hundred-thousand Americans believe that, in reality, the culture of the ancient Indian tribes came from the land of MU."

"What?" Leopold asked. It hit him like a ton of bricks. They all looked at him.

"From the land of MU."

Everyone was silent. After a pause, Leopold said: "Why, that sounds terrible!" He planted his chin in his hand and repeated: "That sounds terrible."

He glanced up and saw how puzzled they all were.

"It sounds like a haunted island – or like the Bermuda Triangle and anti-matter – maybe it is in the Bermuda Triangle," Peter Mattauer decided. Altenweil continued the thought:

"Or like the notorious Black Holes in the universe – quasars, or whatever they call them. The first time I heard of them, it sent shivers down my spine. In every Black Hole an entire universe is supposed to have collapsed into a chunk as big as your fist and has such an enormous density that you can't see it, and it can only emit radio waves – at least that's how I understood it."

"And you're afraid of invisible, fist-sized chunks that emit radio waves?" Peter Mattauer asked, amused.

"Yes – apparently."

"Don't be discouraged, I'm also afraid of giant octopi, although there aren't any in the Attersee."

"Bermuda Triangle, Black Holes – something you fall in," Hornik spoke again in his deep voice that had previously named the ominous land. "In the Ötscher there's a money pit. Untold treasures are supposed to be buried down there. One time a fellow climbed down there to retrieve the treasure. When they finally pulled him back up on the rope, his hair had turned white and he had gone insane."

The others in the group were silent. Their faces registered respect in the presence of the Court Counselor's shuddering. They began to comprehend what he must have felt earlier when he had possibly glimpsed the land of MU. They felt a little better when Altenweil, half-preaching, half-pondering, added: "Perhaps the land of MU is the place where the *boogieman* takes the bad children. It starts where our ability to resist ends – and all we can do is throw ourselves on the floor and close our eyes. It's not necessarily death, clearly, because you can die with dignity. But you can't lie on your stomach with dignity."

Erwin Mattauer bent forward over the table: "That's right, that's exactly right! Death, the way nature has preordained it, is ascension into the circle of our loved ones, our comrades-in-arms, our hunting companions. It is not always sweet and honorable to die for the fatherland, but it is sweet and honorable to die beside a beloved. The *Liebestod* is the most primal destiny for every human being! We don't fear death, we fear the fall into nothingness!"

And Altenweil: "Exactly. We can only escape the fall into the land of MU if we love our families and live happily together with them."

They all exhaled, since they had finally got to hear something edifying, especially Leopold: "Come on, drink up. I've still got some Burgenland wine for us!"

Newerkla praised his first sip: "Hmm, we're sort of like the guests at the wedding feast at Cana – we get the best wine at the end! And now we'll get drunk to boot!" It was a heavy, red wine, a late vintage. Mühlhofer poured a whole glass down his throat, drop by drop, and then refilled his glass.

"Yeah, it's easy for you fellows to talk, you two senior citizens!" Erwin Mattauer addressed the Court Counselor and Altenweil. "You already have your loving and lovable wives! But the rest of us still have to earn our happiness, and till then enjoy the anticipation all the more."

Now they discussed how a man's way of life could best prepare him for marital bliss. Altenweil thought that there were some things to be said for being content with anticipation before marriage: "I know a married couple, and I'm certain that neither one of them had

had sex before their marriage, and it's breathtaking how good their marriage is!"

"That's why they're both constantly out of breath from all their sexual gymnastics," Mühlhofer interrupted, and looked as if he'd just swallowed a fly.

Then something else occurred to Erwin:

"Now's the time when we ought to sing something, a song in honor of our host! What's you favorite song? As far as I know, it's "The blacksmith has a daughter…"

They sang the song. The Court Counselor added, smirking: "Yes, Navratil's even got two daughters, and they probably are anxious to get married off." And then they all started to sing:

> "The Court Counselor has two daughters
> Who'd like to get married.
> Let's go back,
> Let's go back,
> Let's go back to Navratils."

"And what else can we celebrate to honor our host?" Erwin shouted out afterward.

Mühlhofer: "A salamander – a toast!"

"There's a real one over there." The Court Counselor pointed to the bay window.

Mühlhofer got up, supporting himself on the tabletop and the arm of his chair, wobbled over to the bay window, slumped to his knees, reached into the glass bowl and pulled out the salamander. Braced against the wall, he stood up again, wobbled back over to his place, plopped down in his chair, placed the salamander on his plate and held his wineglass over it: "*Ad exercitium salamandris!*"

They all stared at him, bewildered, a bit amused at his wobbling around and also at the salamander who looked so cute as it waddled around on its tiny paws. But a second later Mühlhofer had pressed the edge of the glass down on the plate and the salamander's head was squashed. The remainder of its body, legs, and tail thrashed about desperately. "Be still!" Mühlhofer commanded and severed the salamander's tail. Then he picked it up with two fingers, put it in his wine glass so that it resembled a beaker of formaldehyde, raised his glass and instructed the group: "A *wormus reptilicus*!"

The other guests slowly realized what had just happened and looked over at Leopold Navratil. But he was just sitting there, close-lipped.

"I think it's gotten to be very late," Altenweil said in the midst of the prevailing numbness and stood up. The other guests also got up. Each one shook hands with the Court Counselor, thanked him for the evening, and disappeared out the front door. Leopold had to follow them and unlock the door to the street. Almost in chorus they said "Good night" and were gone.

As Court Counselor Navratil went back up to his apartment he could feel the wine in his head and legs. Upstairs he cast a gloomy glance at the remains on the table, then he turned his back on it, plopped down on the piano bench and opened the lid. He could still hear the dying chords of "Navratil's got two daughters," but he shook it off and played the first notes of Mozart's sonata in A-major. He could hear the apartment door open quietly, and a moment later Maria entered the room, pleasantly surprised by the evening's music. But then she was stunned to discover the squashed salamander. A great weight on her chest pulled her down. She dropped onto the sofa and just sat there, her face buried in her hands. Her father stopped playing, sat down beside her, put his arm around her and hugged her. She remained silent, but the weight on her chest became even greater.

"For God's sake, just tell me what happened?" Erika screamed the next morning.

"It was Mühlhofer," Leopold answered. Aside from this, on that day and the following days, the family said very little.

Court Counselor Navratil phoned Department Head Mattauer: "Hello! Your son, Peter, told me he was interested in an assistant's position at the Socio-Economic Institute, and I promised him that I would talk to Engelhofer about it. Is that all right with you? Actually, I've known Engelhofer since our earliest childhood. We used to throw stones at each other over the fence."

"Why, thank you, that's really very kind of you," Mattauer answered.

Dr. Herbert Engelhofer had given up his law practice a long time ago and had reformed from being a National-Socialist to a Socialist. That had been easy for him when he realized that the National part was just a different manifestation of the Social element – under certain historical conditions, the highest form. He condemned the Nazi crimes against the Jews and dissenters. He recognized that it had been a historic mistake to want to combat bourgeois ideas and bourgeois lifestyles by physically exterminating their proponents instead of by altering their economic foundation. That National Socialism had also turned against other ideologies than just that of the middle-class was of no concern to Engelhofer, since – as he realized in retrospect – he was only interested in suppressing those bourgeois ideologies that had also been suppressed by the Nazis. Today he was sitting at an even nicer desk than he had had formerly in his law practice, and over his desk in place of the Führer hung a portrait of the Empress Maria Theresia, resplendent in all her maternal glory.

On a regular basis Court Counselor Navratil's clerk handed him invitations to lectures, seminars, or other events where articulate speakers intended to persuade others of their opinions on the nation and society. It was his usual custom to read them with grim amusement: it serves you right if you go and listen to this mindless blather! On one of the invitations he had spied Engelhofer's name. He knew where he could find Engelhofer. And he found him.

Court Counselor Navratil entered a deep-freeze that was furnished with plastic chairs and a plastic lectern. Seated in the chairs were longhaired and colorfully seedy students; administrators from various organizations, mostly in gray pinstriped suits; and some old geezers who probably considered themselves intellectuals, some with eyeglasses, some with beards, some with both eyeglasses and beards, and some with neither.

Through the door strode an administrator and, trotting thoughtfully behind him, Engelhofer – tall, stooped, and still blond. The administrator welcomed the audience: "Ladies and Gentlemen, please let me welcome you..." and, as an introduction, observed that the critical awareness of the modern scientist in a future-oriented society has high social status, today more than ever before. And then the moderator was delighted to turn the podium over to the prominent speaker. Engelhofer stepped to the podium, placed a sheet of paper down before him, spoke about methodology, progressivism, and social relevance...and after three-quarters of an hour came to the conclusion that, today more than ever before, the critical awareness of the modern scientist in a future-oriented society has high social status. The audience applauded in moderation, three or four of them posed questions. Then the moderator, who had opened the program, thanked the speaker and the audience, and closed the program.

Court Counselor Navratil allowed the audience to pass by him on their way out the door, and stepped into the path of his Highness, Dr. Social Relevance.

"Hi, Herbert! Remember me?"

Herbert remembered him.

"You can't forget how we studied at the university together and as children tossed rocks at each other over the fence."

He couldn't forget.

"I was thinking I'd learn a little something about modern social- and scientific policies – you gave an interesting lecture."

"Uh-huh, I see."

"I didn't take a very active part in the discussion since I'm basically a beginner on this subject. But I'll keep studying, and next time I'll do all the talking during the discussion."

"Sure, very good."

"By the way, you know our friend and colleague Mattauer, Department Head Mattauer. Of course you know him. His son is presently applying for a vacant assistantship at the Socio-Economic Institute. I was just thinking that if I ran into you, I would mention it to you – maybe you could look at his application in a favorable light. But I don't want to take up any more of your time. See you!"

They shook hands, and Court Counselor Navratil felt himself compelled to make a slight bow; it registered the memory of a time so long ago when he had bowed before Engelhofer. Then he went home.

A few weeks later Court Counselor Navratil left the office for home, as usual, and went into the kitchen to say hello to his wife. She was doing something or other at the kitchen table and didn't even look up. Her lips were pursed, sharp lines descended from the corners of her mouth.

"Hi, how're you doing?"

"Hi. Maria is leaving."

"Leaving? Where's she going?"

"To Düsseldorf."

"To Düsseldorf?"

"With her fiancé, Dr. Sekeli. She wants to marry him. Peter Mattauer got the job at the Institute."

So, that was it. It wasn't what he had intended. It wasn't what he had anticipated. But shouldn't he have been able to anticipate the consequences? In retrospect, he had to admit: yes. It's easy to be smart, in retrospect.

And what, exactly, did Erika know? Why did she emphasize the fact that the Mattauer boy had gotten the job at the Institute? Leopold's brief conversation with Engelhofer couldn't have contributed a great deal to the choice – Department Head Mattauer probably had his own connections. But what was her understanding of the whole thing? He couldn't ask her about it. How could he approach her now? Simply by being silent? He put his arm around her and stroked her back with his hand. What was she feeling at this moment? Suddenly he knew:

She was feeling how something wrapped itself around her and crawled down her back. The crawly thing was the one who had demystified her fairytale prince, thrown her flower elves into a salad bowl, ridiculed her scholarly profession, soiled her clean kitchen every night with his disgusting beer glass, squashed the salamander, and driven their daughter out of the country. Both of them were numb and silent.

He couldn't stand being in her presence any longer and, without saying a word and without knowing why, he went up to the attic.

It had become dark. He didn't turn on the light, but was able to find his way to his partitioned area anyway. He stepped to the window. In the middle of the nocturnal city St. Stephan's cathedral stretched its spine into the starry, clear autumn evening. The black vastness with the eternally incomprehensible stars, which multiplied the longer you looked at them, opened up before him. He gazed down into the courtyard that he knew so well – but deep down. Then back up to the sky and back down into the courtyard. The lights in the windows gradually went out, one by one. Was there peace of mind for him down there in the darkness, or a terrifying fall and a terrifying impact? Shuddering, he stepped back from the window.

He stood alone in the darkness. His daughter was gone, she had slipped away – and with her his paternal pride, his years as a father. His wife was also gone, he couldn't hold her, couldn't get her back – and with her his masculine pride, his years as a man. He stood there alone, as a precarious bachelor. But no, not even alone: out of the fog emerged Mattauer – to whom he had gambled away his life – in uniform, a pistol in his hand; Mattauer charged forward, waved up a column of riflemen, peered out into the field and strode on ahead, over and on past Leopold. In a frantic tumble he plummeted through his life, and it wasn't long before he was standing there, a child, at the beginning of his life, arms and fingers stretching out helplessly into the void, staring up into the darkness.

He could hear a singing in his ears, a slowly increasing crescendo. And then, all of a sudden, it happened:

Ice-cold fear seized his entire body, forced his mouth and eyes wide open, tears plunged down his cheeks –

The darkness was alive, it vibrated with disaster, it crept nearer, it enveloped him. He screamed, screamed without making a sound –

He was in the land of MU!

Erika lay down in the empty bed, breathed deeply, and fell asleep. In her dreamless sleep she could hear the doorbell ringing. From the window she could see the gray of early morning. She yanked herself out of bed, slipped her arms into the sleeves of her dressing gown, and dragged herself over to the door. "Co e quick, Ma'am! Look what's happened!" the landlady wheezed at her. Erika followed the landlady down the stairs to the courtyard gate. The door to the courtyard was open. The landlady stepped aside to let Erika go ahead. She could see the soles of two shoes, the heels pointing upward, then a bundle of clothes from which the shoes emerged, and two arms stretched out on both sides. And then she saw him, lying there, sprawled out – his boyish face pressed into the granite hump of the courtyard pavement as if he were trying to snuggle down between the cobblestones. She saw him again as he once was, her big boy, her rascal, the way he was when she first adored, smiled, hugged, and stroked him, not hidden behind any pompous speeches, a sparse but still unruly lock of hair over his forehead. She could feel her tears coming, knelt down and wanted to take his head in her hands. But his head was cold and positioned stiffly on his neck; she also noticed that his underside had been crushed by the pavement. And now she became horrified of the blood that had run out of his mouth and into the cracks between the cobblestones. She was startled and caught sight of the open attic window – it revealed some things to her and concealed a great deal more. And while she ran her fingers through Leopold's hair, she looked up, still higher, into the grayness, to the ice through which he had broken.

Afterword

For a foreigner attempting to understand Austrian culture and institutions, nothing could be more mundane and yet typically Austrian than the civil service. Over the years natives and foreigners alike have been entertained or horrified by stories of the intransigence, the inertia, the unresponsiveness and intractability of the Austrian bureaucracy. If we assume that the novels of Franz Kafka – especially *The Trial* and *The Castle* – are based on the modern bureaucracies he encountered in twentieth century Austria, we can gain some idea of their opaque and imposing sovereignty, their unapproachable almost hostile nature.

What better guide through the idiosyncrasies of the Austrian bureaucracy than a lifetime civil servant and diplomat like Georg Potyka. He was born in Vienna on 30 April 1938, studied Law in Vienna and at Tulane University in New Orleans, entering the diplomatic service in 1961. He was posted to India, Pakistan, and the Netherlands, and has served as the Austrian ambassador to Iraq and Bulgaria. His service has included an assignment to the Foreign Ministry in Vienna, primarily in the office for International Law, and as director of the department for International Environmental Protection. In these capacities, he participated in numerous inter-national negotiations and conferences.

Georg Potyka's publications include feuilletons, short stories, and legal treatises, the novel *Lebenswette* [A Life's Wager] (1995), a reference book on law making and decision-making in international law, *Rechtsetzung und Entscheidung im Völkerrecht* [Making Laws and Decisions in International Law] (2000), as well as a book of political essays with a satirical flavor, *Vielbeschimpftes Österreich* [Much Ado about Austria] (2002). He has two honorary degrees, one from the University of Plovdiv and another from the Music Academy in Sofia. Married with four children, Dr. Potyka is now retired and resides in Maria Enzersdorf outside Vienna.

An Overview of the Austrian Civil Service

Seemingly since time immemorial, bureaucracies have been a

requisite structure for law and order, for administering the affairs of state, both foreign and domestic. Empires from ancient Greece and Rome to ancient China produced forms of civil service to ensure communication, implementation, and administration of imperial decrees in their far-flung realms. Thus from the outset the Holy Roman Empire under Charlemagne required extensive organization. When the Austrian Habsburgs ascended the throne of the Empire in 1273, they, too, would continue and later expand the development of a civil service that was to provide the services necessary to guarantee political and social stability and prosperity.

An administrative structure required literate and obedient representatives, servants of the state who could read and write and implement the decisions of the Emperor and his advisors. Any and all aspects of life would ultimately be involved: from road-building to sanitation, from conscription of soldiers to levying of taxes, from the regulation of commerce to the standardization of laws, education. With the gradual disintegration of the feudal system and the advent of the Enlightenment, a more effective, more sophisticated bureaucracy became possible. The Age of Reason and its proponents in Austria, beginning with Maria Theresa, encouraged modernization of a cumbersome civil service with the intention of providing rational, consistent, and thoughtful governance. As one scholar has observed: "A feature of the Habsburg Monarchy until the reforms of Maria Theresa was the lack of a graded bureaucracy and a class of government officials."[1]

By 1740 reforms were becoming evident; new councils, departments, committees, as well as provincial governments flourished, with a corresponding increase in personnel. "At the same time, norms of administrative practice were tentatively introduced, along with regular salary scales, recognizable career paths, some pension expectations (if not rights), elements of training for the public service, and a new esprit de corps.[2]

The challenge of the Habsburgs derived from the composition

---

[1] Robert Birely, S.J., "Confessional Absolutism in the Habsburg lands in the Seventeenth Century," in Charles, W. Ingrao, ed., *State and Society in Early Modern Austria* (West Lafayette, IN: Purdue University Press, 1994), 9.
[2] R.J.W.Evans, "Introduction: State and Society in Early Modern Austria," in Charles, W. Ingrao, ed., *State and Society in Early Modern Austria* (West Lafayette, IN: Purdue University Press, 1994), 9.

of their empire. They ruled over many lands, each with its own unique customs, laws, privileges and often featuring a non-Austrian populace with its own distinct language and culture.³

Nevertheless the government's representatives were, of necessity, German speakers, steeped in Austrian traditions. That the Habsburgs were able to acquire and rule a world empire, primarily through diplomacy, marriage, and political alliances rather than through war and conquest, became a matter of national pride.

By the middle of the eighteenth century, Maria Theresa had introduced various governmental reforms based on enlightened principles. She not only expanded the size of the military to keep pace with her European rivals, a second army of civil servants was enlisted to efficiently govern her many territories. Over the next forty years the size of the civil service would more than triple.⁴

With the death of Maria Theresa in 1780, her son Joseph II fully assumed the title of Holy Roman Emperor and thus the sole leadership of the Empire. His intended reforms were even more progressive and far-reaching than those of his mother, ultimately earning the all-encompassing appellation "Josephinism." Superficially, his uniform code of centralization and consolidation required that his representatives wear uniforms as well. A primary objective was to infuse the administration with his own dedication to the state: "One early measure introduced the Prussian system of annual reports on officials' performance by their superiors; another granted them automatic pension rights. Material gain was not, however, to be the primary incentive. In a famous circular of 1783 Joseph wrote that Austria needed men able to renounce all life's pleasures for the sake of the public weal."⁵

In short, he wanted to create a bureaucracy that was based on merit and loyalty, and not on birth. For this reason, educational qualifications were gradually instituted for the various ranks, and university training became a fast track to an appointment in the civil service. "The law continued to enjoy immense prestige. Around half

---

³ See Charles W. Ingrao, *The Habsburg Monarchy* 1618-1815, 2ⁿᵈ ed. (Cambridge: Cambridge University Press, 2000), 245.

⁴ According to Ingrao, *The Habsburg Monarchy*, 1618-1815, 164-165.

⁵ Robin Okey, *The Habsburg Monarchy: From Enlightenment to Eclipse* (New York: St. Martin's Press, 2001), 41.

of Austria's university students studied it, for it was the basic degree for a career in public life; the succession of able, legally trained bureaucrats of at least mildly liberal views and reformist plans who figured in public life" was an intended result of Joseph's civil service reforms.[6]

Joseph's improvements were retained into the nineteenth century, modified and improved as the times dictated. "The Basic Laws of 1867... gave the interpretation of legal texts an important place in political life; indeed, it may be said that the attempt to devise legal answers to political problems was a characteristic feature of Austrian political life."[7]

On a practical level, the bulk of civil servants were poorly paid, with a commensurate level of performance: they spent fewer than eight hours a day at their posts and were not known to expedite the matters of state. As one scholar notes, the wheels of state moved "often grindingly slowly but on the whole benevolently and competently. True, attempts to speed them up made little headway, despite a major inquest of 1911, which found that nearly a third of officials sampled processed one file a day or less."[8]

By the onset of the First World War, the civil service regulations, or *Dienstpragmatik*, of 1914 provided the following clarification: "The law distinguishes federal employees (officials), employees by contract, and (state) workers. Federal employees are full-time public officials. Their appointments are regulated by law and they have an indeterminate tenure of office." Similar civil service regulations standardized the duties, obligations, and benefits of the civil service and were later augmented by the federal constitution of 1920 and further amendments over the years.[9]

After centuries of evolution, the resulting bureaucracy consisted of individual civil servants, each with a proscribed area of competency that he must not overstep; petitions beyond his narrow range of responsibility must be referred to superiors for adjudication – the dreaded predicament in which the petitioner can only suffer a

---

[6] Okey, 278.

[7] Okey, 278.

[8] Okey, 340.

[9] Ludwig Maier, "The Austrian Civil Service," in *The Civil Service in the Modern State: A Collection of Documents*, ed. By Leonard D. White (Chicago: University of Chicago Press, 1930), 457.

protracted wait and someday hope for a settlement from on high. Thus the Austrian national characteristic of resignation, obviously perpetuated by the daily encounter with a sluggish bureaucracy, is frequently characterized by two adages: "Glücklich ist, wer vergisst, was nicht mehr zu ändern ist" – Happy is he who can forget what he can't change, from the *Fledermaus*; and "Die Lage ist hoffnungslos, aber nicht ernst" – The situation is hopeless, but not serious.

The Novel

By the beginning of the twentieth century the Austrian civil service had guaranteed its citizens (such as our fictional Leopold Navratil) a predictable, responsible, and efficient system of government which generated a climate of stability and security; a further stabilizing factor was, of course, the presence of an Emperor, Franz Joseph, who had been on the throne for over fifty years – three generations of Austrians were accustomed to seeing his portrait in all aspects of their daily lives, from the stamps on their letters to his framed likeness in post offices and school rooms. The milieu we encounter in the novel is, historically, that which Stefan Zweig portrayed so vividly in his memoir *The World of Yesterday*, a Zeitgeist he so aptly labeled "The Golden Age of Security":

> Everything in our almost thousand-year-old Austrian monarchy seemed based on permanency, and the State itself was the chief guarantor of this stability... Our currency, the Austrian crown, circulated in bright gold pieces, an assurance of its immutability. Everyone knew how much he possessed or what he was entitled to, what was permitted and what forbidden. Everything had its norm, its definite measure and weight... An official or an officer, for example, could confidently look up in the calendar the year when he would be advanced in grade, or when he would be pensioned... No one thought of wars, of revolutions, or revolts. All that was radical, all violence, seemed impossible in an age of reason. This feeling of security was the most

eagerly sought-after possession of millions, the common ideal of life.[10]

This then was the universe into which young Leopold Navratil is born. His world is comprised of naive optimism and youthful expectations, of idealism and fantasy. From childhood he imagines adventure, success, and glory as the namesake of Saint Leopold or Duke Leopold, driving off the Protestants or the Huns with his heroic exploits. His youthful courage is make-believe and always manifests itself under the protective eyes of his parents. But while his imaginary worlds include America, Africa, and the North Pole, the shadow of the threatening unknown hovers over them, up in the darkness of the attic as the ineffable, mysterious, threatening unknown in life – the boogieman. More frightening than the devil, this dread has no shape or size, no recognizable form which could be exorcised. Worse, his mother, one adult he expects to protect him from all threatening entities, reinforces his instinctive timidity of this unknown presence by inculcating his fear of the boogieman, later attempting to endow his daughters with the same phobia.

Leopold can easily imagine the demise of his childhood adversaries: the Huns and the Protestants, and other make-believe enemies; even the neighborhood bully Engelhofer can be avoided, if necessary. Nothing in Leopold's fantasy, however, can prepare him for the unimaginable evil of the Nazis – unlike the Huns of his youthful fantasy, they cannot be dispelled by merely imagining them away. Even his father becomes vulnerable: as an insurance man who was supposed to protect people so that nothing bad could happen to them, he ultimately could not protect his own family or even himself, and he is killed in an air raid.

As we have seen in Zweig, the acquisition of security, both in his profession and in his family life, is of the utmost importance. Though from an unassuming middle-class family, Leopold was able to join the civil service due to his education and abilities, a sinecure which he was to enjoy until his untimely death. He also acquires a wife and two daughters to solidify his personal life and act as a buffer to protect

---

[10] Stefan Zweig, *The World of Yesterday* (Lincoln, NE: University of Nebraska Press, 1964), 1-2.

him from the vicissitudes of life.[11]

Interestingly, since he is dedicated to his post, he takes little notice of world events until or unless they affect his own narrow corner of the Austrian Empire: little explicit mention is made of the newly formed Republic, of the Anschluß, of World War II, or the subsequent establishment of the Second Republic. He obviously notices the Nazi flags in Vienna, the emigration of the Jewish Lemnitzer family, the necessity of cooperation with the new Nazi regime, and, of course, he eventually is forced to play an active part in the war effort in an anti-aircraft battery. But his actions are unreflective, more a product of his limited survival skills. Like a good and loyal bureaucrat, he focuses on his narrowly defined tasks within the civil service and in his personal life, and takes few unauthorized risks. Of course, on closer inspection, the society and the civil service are contradictory in nature: Navratil mentions the impact of Emperor Joseph II's reforms at the end of the eighteenth century as "a representative of that enlightened Austria that thinks in aphorisms, that abolished censorship under Joseph II and reinstated it under Metternich, that promises all freedoms and proscribes the funeral rites" (139). Leopold prefers to ignore such contradictions and impediments to the normal course of affairs within his department. He seeks established norms and thus security within the institution.

Still, as an adult, his rivals and enemies are not so easily dismissed: David Richardson, Philipp Mattauer, and the bully Herbert Engelhofer, his daughter's suitor Dr. Sekeli. Threats to Navratil's domestic security are met either with suspicion, jealousy...and ultimately with paralysis. His rage at Americans stems from his rivalry

---

[11] Some critics would perhaps see in Leopold Navratil's anxious vulnerability the plight of Europe's middle classes following the Great War, as they attempt to find some security in a world of constant changes, many of which are threatening or incomprehensible. See Jacques Barzun, *From Dawn to Decadence: 500 Years of Western Cultural Life* (New York: HarperCollins, 2000), when he describes "family life broken as badly as by divorce; careers, occupations ended and livelihood reduced to a meager government allowance; social distinctions and manners diluted or erased – even clothing and speech altered to fit new human relations, loss of bourgeois pride and comforts..." (708). Peter Gay notes the ideal of work as a buffer against change: "It implied honest dealings with employers, customers, and competitors, a dedication to self-discipline, a wholesome commitment to family, and an alert sense of duty." In: *Schnitzler's Century: The Making of Middle-Class Culture 1815-1914* (New York: Norton, 2002), 192.

with the American exchange student David Richardson, increases with the war, and continues in peacetime when his wife is enamored with American ideals such as democracy and a humane educational system (and exhibits David's postcards as symbols of a competing lifestyle – perhaps also of an idealized suitor). This explains Leopold's disdain for Americans and things American, since he sees them as powerful, thoughtful, creative, spontaneous – qualities he does not possess and thus mistrusts; he understands a dictator like Stalin, but not a president like Roosevelt. It is instructive that Leopold envies their prevailing ideals and their success, since his ideals were destroyed and his bravery remains elusive.

He ultimately destroys his own family circle by patronizing Mattauer's son in place of his future son-in-law Dr. Sekeli; because Sekeli is from outside his social and professional circle, Leopold immediately assumes the worst and imagines the stranger to be a smuggler or crook. And in one instance he is simply paralyzed, when he is ill prepared for the violence against his daughter's salamander and can do nothing to prevent it. The death of the fragile pet simultaneously represents the demise of his tenuous family bonds.

Verticality

Within a bureaucracy as in society at large, there is an obvious, proscribed hierarchy that attains a dimension of verticality in the novel. This vertical perspective is seen throughout Navratil's life. At an early age Leopold is frightened by the prospect of climbing up to the attic, a height to which he is unaccustomed, and which is simultaneously identified as the lair of the boogieman. Later he experiences looking up to the spires of St. Stephan's cathedral, only to be overcome by dizziness in the face of his insignificance. His fear of heights is a motif repeated throughout the novel, a fear both realistic and symbolic, and it is in the crucial wager that he attempts to drag Mattauer down into the (wine) cellar with him where he perceives life to be safe and unthreatening. By extension, any ascending fortune in life such as a career promotion or the establishment of a family, the birth of children, etc., is always jeopardized by the possibility of loss, in vertical terms, of a fall. Falling into the land of MU, into the abyss, signifies the loss of his hard-won professional, physical, social, emotional, and existential security, down into the depths, simultaneously an admission of his failure in life. (Paradoxically, and on a humorous note, two benefits accrue on the horizontal scale: with the death of Leopold's mother, the family is able to spread out into the vacated space; as for Leopold himself, he remarks that the one horizontal movement in his adult life is the expansion of his waistline, the traditional visual confirmation of his success as Court Counselor.)

During this tumultuous period, all of the novel's individual characters experience life in a vertical plane of ups and downs, both professionally and personally. There is no horizontal movement where the characters, for example, leave Austria; indeed, they seldom venture far from Vienna. It is only the desperate, like the Jewish Lemnitzer family, who must emigrate (significantly, to America). While Rosi and her family are able to escape the Old World's stratification, Nazi rule, and even almost certain extermination by moving in a horizontal plane – crossing geographic and nationalistic boundaries to arrive at a new life in the New World – few of her Austrian acquaintances are willing or able to attempt such a drastic move. As is fitting for a life dedicated to a hierarchical structure such as the civil service, Leopold Navratil moves in a vertical plane and thus cannot deviate from this dimension. He and his rivals Mattauer and Engelhofer must remain in Austria and make accommodations to whatever political system prevails, be it republican, fascist, socialist, or democratic.

The Wager

Leopold's wager with Mattauer is a pivotal yet curious event. Although they are not explicitly competing with one another, there is a social hierarchy represented, in descending order, by Mattauer, Navratil, and eventually Engelhofer. The wager is related to Navratil's fear of vulnerability, related to his envy of Mattauer the man, but also to Leopold's pride. And his related need to prove that his worth as a man and a civil servant is commensurate with that of his peers. Several times he must bow before Mattauer and Engelhofer, indicating his subservience to them. To balance this shame, he must reestablish his own self-worth by demonstrating, for example, that Mattauer is on his level, thus susceptible to the laws of Leopold's concept of verticality. Yet their different backgrounds and philosophies do not lend themselves to comparison. Mattauer is wealthy, with good social contacts, and thus can risk putting himself above the law with his political activities; Leopold comes from a more modest upbringing, fostering his innate desire to support the law – it is his cushion against chaos such as that caused by the Nazis. Navratil's wager is therefore unrealistic, as is his attempt to humble Mattauer and bring him down to Navratil's level.

Regardless of their differences, each must come to terms with the changing times, occasioned by the Nazis' annexation of their Austrian homeland. Mattauer barely survives with his code of honor; Navratil compromises for his and his family's sake; Engelhofer, the bully, is a natural fascist and clever enough to weasel his way into the good graces of the Socialists after the war. The Mattauers of the world can always withdraw to their private estates and survive quietly with their own resources; the Engelhofers can always land on their feet due to their resilience and lack of principle, whereas the Navratils must bend or break, since they have neither the independent wealth which would allow them to withdraw from conflict nor the brutality to combat their opponents. Leopold's wager, then, is not a Faustian pact with the Devil but an unspoken challenge to another complicated human being (who is completely unaware that there is, in fact, any wager at all). Finally, Leopold wishes to promote Mattauer's son, certainly to curry Mattauer's favor and debt, but also to embarrass the man, to force him to disclose his innermost thoughts and principles. In the end, Leopold does not know Mattauer, does not know what he has suffered or what he is thinking, yet nevertheless assumes Mattauer has "won" the silent wager.

A further aspect of the wager concerns their differing concepts of the law – thus representing their competence within the civil service – a dispute that Leopold hopes to win by convincing Mattauer by superior reasoning and the force of his convictions. A pointed example of these philosophical differences arises during their dispute regarding the law and an attractive female petitioner, Dr. Ildiko Bakos. Leopold rules by the letter of the law and therefore must deny her claim; Mattauer, his superior, is personally attracted to the charming woman and finds a loophole in the law that will allow her petition. In the ensuing discussion between the two, Mattauer is sensitive to the stolidity of the bureaucracy, attempting to inject a bit of human sympathy into the proceedings. Leopold counters that Mattauer has effectively bypassed the law, making their work subjective, thus anarchical. Mattauer responds that Leopold is overreacting – that law and order was nonexistent under the Nazis and that now Leopold is attempting to make the law all-pervasive – at least as great a threat as that of the Nazis. The encounter prompts Leopold to undertake a study of legal decision-making. His public address on that topic exposes the lack of checks and balances between the ministries; his allusion to the civil servant who can implement a pet project by dodging his superiors is clearly aimed at Mattauer. It is, however, a show of farce, since Leopold does not follow through with an official complaint – again he has bowed before superior force and will not challenge the hierarchy above him. Their debate touches on a critical issue of historic importance for all citizens: what should be the primary objective of the civil service, order or compassion, as represented by Navratil and Mattauer respectively? In truth, as Navratil discovers, the bureaucracy is out of control, no checks and balances exist, since Mattauer can basically do whatever he can get away with. With Leopold's failure to counter Mattauer's apparent anarchy in the office, his defeat within his family only seals his fate. It is this conclusive recognition of his pervasive impotence that drives him to his death. Sadly, we must wonder if Leopold could even have a "wager," when the other party is completely unaware of the bet or of the stakes?

Leopold's personal crisis is reiterated in the philosophies expressed by his young fraternity brothers, the sons of his peers. Young Newerkla expresses his conviction that men are incomplete without women, and that a man tends to seek a woman like his mother (p. 125). After his marriage, Leopold is torn between his allegiance to the two women in his life: his mother now lives with them and competes with his wife Erika for his attention and support. Leopold's mother propagates the boogieman for him and for his daughters (here in opposition to his wife); Leopold's weak attempt to placate them and to avoid conflict satisfies neither woman. Furthermore, Leopold can also identify with the thoughts of young Mattauer and he is inspired by his concept of the *Liebestod* (p. 126) where man is redeemed at death by the love his family has for him. Despite all his external successes, in the end Leopold learns that he is a superfluous member of his own family and that his wife could possibly leave him. Leopold can only assume that there is no love for him after the chaos he has created in his family by supporting Mattauer's son for a position that could have gone to his prospective son-in-law Dr. Sekeli. Erika is repulsed by his touch, his dirty beer glass, his war books, so that he could realistically expect that his marriage is over – though Erika's reaction upon seeing him dead might lead us to believe otherwise.

Expansion and Augmentation

With all the emphasis on the two men, their careers, crises, and successes, their lives gain in significance when seen against the backdrop of the time. Vignettes of peripheral characters offer a variety of representative reactions, from a loyal Nazi officer to a pragmatic soldier, from an opportunistic teacher to a radical engineer, as well as the inevitable victims of Nazi tyranny and the war. Minor figures, such as the competent and courageous senior Mattauer and his wife, provide a rich setting for the travails of our main characters.

Yet even more revealing are the depictions of contemporary women. Though they may have professional lives, as teachers for example, we are shown women primarily as wives and partners. The question of "ownership" which Erika raises, highlights the subservient role of wives within a patriarchic tradition which is gradually superceded in the new, democratic Austria with roles for independent women. Christine Mattauer is a true helpmate who takes an equal part in running their farm, while conspiring with her husband in the resistance to the Nazis. Dr. Trude Kulnik, an independent and mature professional, chooses to marry an engineer and begin a new life on equal footing with her husband. Erika, as the wife of our main character, proves to be a fascinating figure. She loves her husband, in spite of his many attempts to control her life and thoughts, and can choose to embark on her own life as a teacher, rejecting "ownership" of Leopold while resisting his attempts to "own" or dominate her. In a notable move, she is able to refurbish a corner of the kitchen as her own workspace, thereby establishing her independence as a member of the family, as a professional, and as a human being.

Of special interest is her eldest daughter Maria as a representative of the younger generation. Strikingly, Maria rejects both of her father's preferred suitors, apparently because they share the selfsame philosophies of her father. Unlike the gregarious Leopold, she quietly chooses, instead, a modest young businessman who wants to redistribute the world's goods while sharing his life with her. She also resists her father's concept of verticality, in that she willingly leaves Austria for Germany to follow her future husband. She seems a thoughtful, sensitive young woman who appears able to overcome any inherent shortcomings from her father and consequently provides hope for the future.

In conclusion, through the multitude of characters portrayed, we can recognize several responses to the loss of law and order, of tradition and security as a result of the Nazi takeover and, later, with the advent of a "new" normalcy. The teacher and Engelhofer are opportunists – the teacher is shot trying to surrender, while Engelhofer is able to adapt to the new order; Mattauer is, of course, a quasi-hero here, suffering for his ideals and secretly supporting the resistance movement, though on a small scale, by providing food for endangered persons. Leopold is none of the above and must navigate a different course; a product of his youthful fantasies and the Austrian bureaucracy he so diligently serves, he is too idealistic to convert to National Socialism, too unimaginative to resist; in this clash he has meager resources at his disposal and must attempt to survive as best he can. But it is in the ensuing peacetime, in the increasing prosperity and seeming security of middle-age that he ultimately fails. As in the war, he is now ill-prepared for success. He can hide behind his bureaucratic activities in the office and then attempt to hide at home with his glass of beer, his books on war, and his imagined vassals. But he has failed to fulfill his boyhood fantasies of courage and glory. More importantly he has failed to accommodate the changing needs within his family, assuming that as paterfamilias he alone can pilot the family's destiny – and that in doing so he automatically deserves respect and obedience. In the end is alone and lonely, a failure in his own eyes. He is not a pathetic figure, but certainly a cautionary one. In short, the reader should realize that despite Leopold Navratil's distinct Austrian heritage, his unique profession, and his singular personality, he is merely one of us.

Todd C. Hanlin